Prai

"*From Where We Are* is a multi-generational punch-to-the-heart reminder that there is no such thing as a singular Jewish experience. It is our collective experience—regardless of religion, gender, physical or mental ability, ethnicity, sexual orientation, or any aspect of our diverse world—from which we can learn, be better, and do better."

JEFFREY DALE LOFTON, AWARD-WINNING AUTHOR OF *RED CLAY SUZIE*

"A sensitive exploration of contemporary Jewish history, *From Where We Are* charts the effects of intergenerational trauma, and its unfolding through the lives of one beautiful, complex family."

RABBI ANDRUE KAHN, EDITOR OF
SACRED EARTH: JEWISH PERSPECTIVES ON OUR PLANET

"A kaleidoscopic gem that adeptly showcases how the shameful misdeeds of the past reverberate into modern acts of violence... Zelniker pulls us into a sweeping, multigenerational saga of family ties, resilience, and the tenacity of the human spirit in healing the wounds of our traumas... An emotional tour de force."

DAVID JACKSON AMBROSE, AUTHOR OF *UNLAWFUL DISORDER*

"A layered excavation of intergenerational trauma and a perceptive probe into how resilience can overcome it... Zelniker's sympathetic and complex characters offer diverse answers to the question posed by one survivor, 'Can we ever escape the shadows of those who came before us?' Zelniker's response is a moving evocation of an extended family united by history, memory, re-invention, and hope."

ANN S. EPSTEIN, AUTHOR OF *THE SISTER KNOT*

About the Author

Nicole Zelniker (she/they) is the author of several books, including *Until We Fall*, which was a finalist for the Forward Indie Awards in LGBTQ+ adult fiction. She's also the founder and editor-in-chief of the literary magazine *Knee Brace Press*. In her free time, Nicole enjoys re-reading her favorite books, listening to musicals, and bothering her cat.

nicolezelniker.com

from
where

we
are

nicole
zelniker

www.vineleavespress.com

From Where We Are
Copyright © 2024 Nicole Zelniker

All rights reserved.
Print Edition
ISBN: 978-3-98832-118-3
Published by Vine Leaves Press 2024

Cover design by Jessica Bell
Interior design by Amie McCracken

For the millions who died,
the millions who lived,
and all who came after.

"All the good you have accomplished will continue
in the lives of the people you have touched ...
Everything is connected, like a chain that cannot be broken."
Eva Schloss, author of *Eva's Story* and *The Promise*, a survivor

"You have no control who lives,
who dies,
who tells your story."
Christopher Jackson, *Hamilton*

Author's Note

From Where We Are contains subject matter that can be difficult for some readers, like characters struggling with their mental health, discrimination against marginalized groups, on page violence, and more. I've included all of this because in writing a story about intergenerational trauma and state-sanctioned violence, it felt disingenuous to shy away from these topics.

As always, readers should always prioritize their mental health and if you're not ready for this story, that's ok. It will be here when you are.

For a full list of content warnings, please head to nicolezelniker.com/from-where-we-are.

Chapter One: Kindergarten
1922-1955

The day they came for her brother, Gabi's world shattered. It had held firm through dwindling food stores and yellow notices in the Jewish-owned bakeries her family often frequented. It held through splintered window storefronts along the blocks the men in her family traversed to get to work and the seemingly overnight rejection by her neighbors and former friends. It held through the day her nephew came home crying because he wasn't allowed to play with his classmates in the park anymore and the men chasing her husband down the street because he was a "dirty Jew" and "communist scum."

Gabi's world lasted until they came for Eli, and then everything fell apart.

They needed, big, strong men, they said. Eli's son Fritz, just thirteen years old at the time, barely qualified as a child. It helped that he was small for his age. Eli's younger son, Albert, who had always looked older than his nine years. Gabi thanked God he was too young, even though she wasn't sure anymore if God existed.

Her husband Wally, who worked at the university, got a pass for now. But they would be back, Mama said. "You have to leave."

Gabi and Wally sat at Mama's kitchen table, the room clean but nearly empty after so long rationing their food supplies. They visited Mama often, their own house just two blocks north and just as bare of sustenance. Gabi and Wally held hands under the table.

"We can't leave," Gabi said. "This is our home." Gabi had never been to anywhere beyond Germany except for Hungary, where she once visited her sister-in-law's parents on holiday with her brother. Even then, she'd been relieved to come home after that trip, grateful to wake in her own bed the following morning.

"They'll come for Wally next," Mama insisted. "And then they'll come for you."

Gabi knew she was right, even if she didn't want to says so. Already, they heard frantic whispers when they passed through town, harried murmurs of death in the work camps where they had supposedly taken Eli. Gabi didn't believe half of them, and she chose not to believe the more frightening ones, like the rooms full of poison gas, but they couldn't all be lies.

"Wally, what do you think?" Mama asked. The yellow star of David stood out starkly against her black sleeve, stitches sloppy along the seams.

Wally took off his round, black-rimmed glasses and rubbed them on his shirt once, twice, three times. He put them back on and pushed them up his nose. "I think we have to leave," he murmured.

Gabi pulled her hand from Wally's, her cheeks flushed with anger and the energy she expended trying desperately not to cry. "How could you say that?"

"They'll take us," Wally said. "And then we won't have a home at all."

"How can we not fight this?" Gabi asked. "How—"

"My mausi, you will be fighting," Mama said. "You'll survive."

Gabi's jaw clenched. Tears pricked at her eyes, and she blinked quickly to keep them from falling. "Well, you have to come with us."

"Not without Eli," Mama said. "I'll stay for Eli."

"We'll find him then," Gabi said, her throat tight. "We'll find out where he went and—"

Mama shook her head. "No." Their eyes met, and Gabi realized what Mama already knew. Eli was gone to them forever, and if Mama stayed behind, she would be gone to Gabi too.

Gabi swallowed around the lump in her throat. She looked at Wally, who nodded, and turned back to Mama. "How?"

.

Walking home with Wally that evening, Gabi took everything in. It was light, still, but the street she'd grown up on seemed perpetually dark with fear. Her mama's neighbors, mostly Jewish, stayed inside these days. All throughout Gabi's youth, she couldn't peer out her front door without waving hello to Mrs. Schwartz on her way home from temple in the evening or seeing Mr. Wasserman hurry down the street, briefcase in hand. Now, it had been so long since she had seen anyone she'd known back then, not in the least because half of them had already fled. Even the church at the end of their block, ironically placed on such a Jewish street, appeared eerily empty, its windows pitch dark.

Wally squeezed her hand, and Gabi looked over at him. Up at him, rather. Her husband was nearly a head taller, taller than even Eli. He shot up some time around their thirteenth year, around the same age as her elder nephew now. Before that, she could always count on him to be one of the shortest in their class. He'd always been thin, too, but now his cheeks sunk into his skin, hollowing his face. His shirt hung off his skeletal frame. Gabi looked no better.

On their own street, which was more mixed in terms of religion, the family from across the way and two doors down came up the sidewalk from the other side. The father tapped the eldest, Else, a girl of around nine, on the shoulder and whispered something in her ear. Else made eye contact with Gabi and glared daggers with her wide blue eyes. Gabi's own eyes watered, but she turned away before Else and her father could see. Before everything, Gabi had been friendly with her neighbors. They swapped recipes for apple strudel and stories about their childhoods. They exchanged congratulations when someone had a birthday or a graduation and condolences when a relative passed or, more and more often lately, someone in their families lost a job.

Inside, Gabi locked the door behind her. They never used to do that either. She turned to Wally and said, "I suppose it isn't really home anymore anyway."

Wally only nodded, his eyes fixed on the air over Gabi's shoulder, his mind at work mapping out an increasingly unknowable future for them both. Gabi had loved Wally nearly her whole life, but right now, she hated how willing he was to leave the people they cherished most behind.

·

Eli's wife Susan came to their home the day before Gabi and Wally planned to cross the border.

"You need to take Fritz," she said before Gabi could even offer her a seat in the living room. They stood huddled in the foyer, speaking in hushed voices even though no one could hear them. Normally, Gabi would have offered tea as well (both women shared an affinity for hot beverages), but they hadn't had any tea bags in quite a while.

Gabi stared at Susan and said, "You want me to take your son?"

"Albert, he's fair," Susan said. "I can take him back to Hungary. He can pass for a non-Jew, but Fritz can't. I can't risk it. I can't send him to die, Gabi, I can't." Her voice broke, and she turned away. Her beautiful sky-blue eyes stared out the window, at Gabi's neighbor's scurrying down the street.

Susan was right. Fritz had darker features, like Eli and the rest of Gabi's family. Albert had gotten Susan's straw-colored hair and bright blue eyes. It had caused quite a scandal in the community when Eli had married a non-Jew from Hungary, especially after everyone had been so convinced he would marry his childhood sweetheart Goldie, but Goldie's family had moved away at the start of all this. Besides, Mama hadn't minded. She loved Susan and had even given Eli her grandmother's engagement ring, since Gabi would wear Mama's dress for her own wedding to Wally.

"Fritz can't be my son," Gabi said. "He's already a teenager." Eli was ten years older than Gabi, thirty-four to Gabi's twenty-four. She was only eleven years older than Fritz.

"Then say he's younger," Susan said. "He can pass. Or that he's your brother. Say anything."

"How will we find you?" Gabi asked. "After?"

Susan gave Gabi a smile. She sniffed and wiped her eyes on the edge of her frayed sleeve. "My dear sister," she said. "I don't know that there will be an after."

When Gabi and Wally arrived in the dark, and Susan told her children what would happen, Albert, the younger of the two, burst into tears. He cried harder when Gabi, Wally, and Fritz said goodbye. The three of them stood in Eli and Susan's living room at just past midnight. Each of them had one suitcase. They couldn't risk taking too much, not when they would have to pretend to be on holiday once they reached the ship. They were already using false passports and clothes that weren't theirs, provided by Gabi's friend Otto, who'd joined the SS for this very purpose. She worried for him every day.

Albert clung to Fritz and begged him to stay through jagged breaths and heart-wrenching sobs. Fritz told Albert he loved him, then gently pulled himself from his brother's grasp. This was far too much for any of them. Fritz was so young, too young to be torn from his father and mother and brother. Gabi couldn't imagine all she would have missed had she been forced to flee at such a young age.

They walked out the door together, Gabi's heart in her mouth. She had to keep herself from crying, too, for what seemed like the hundredth time this month. Emotions were high, true, but she couldn't help but think she might have been a little stronger had she some food in her stomach.

Years later, when Gabi was pregnant for the first time with her elder daughter, she would replay this moment over and over in her mind. Gabi was nearly thirty when her doctor told her in English. She had been an American for six years.

"What is it?" she asked in her adopted language. "Is it a boy or a girl?"

The doctor laughed. "It's too early to tell," he said. "But it seems healthy, whatever it is."

Gabi put her hands on her stomach. A baby. And then, she felt it sharp and sudden, as she always did. A longing for Mama, whom at this point she hadn't spoken to since she left Germany all those years prior.

"Oh, ma'am, are you all right?" the doctor asked, fiddling with the stethoscope around his neck.

"Yes, yes, sorry," she said, wiping tears from her eyes. "I am just excited." That seemed to be the right answer. The doctor smiled at her, at least, but Gabi couldn't help but think of Fritz and Albert's last goodbye, of the goodbye she never got with Eli.

Gabi always thought she and Wally would have so many children, enough to fill a whole house. In her youth, she'd dreamed of it so often, spent classes daydreaming about the future they would give their babies. A boy for Wally and a girl for her, though the order didn't matter, followed by at least four more. They would take family trips to picnic in the countryside and she would teach them how to read from her favorite books. But now, so many years removed from a time where she could dream so freely, Gabi had seen what could happen to siblings wrenched apart.

She kept this to herself when she told Wally of her pregnancy. "A baby," he said in German. "I'm going to be a father."

"The doctor doesn't know if it's a boy or a girl," Gabi told him in the same language. Always felt a relief to speak it, like she had been treading water and finally reached the shore.

"It doesn't matter," Wally said, his face split nearly in half by his grin. "I'm going to love them so much, no matter what they are, really." He took Gabi's face in his hands and kissed her. Gabi pulled away, laughing. Thoughts of her brother and for her nephews hid in the back of her mind, but they refused to dissipate entirely.

"We'll need to buy baby things," she said, gesturing to their apartment. It was two rooms, one for them and one for Fritz, and a joint kitchen and living room. The paint on the thin walls was cracked and scuffed. The only bathroom was in the hall, shared by the floor.

"It doesn't matter," Wally said. "We'll find a way. I'll work more jobs."

Gabi gave him a small smile. In Germany, Wally had worked at the university, teaching writing to bright-eyed students who hung on his every word. In America, Wally washed cars.

—

Before everything changed, before her family was wrenched apart and her life was irrevocably, undeniably, and devastatingly altered, Gabi Altenberg loved learning. At five years old, she loved reading, but never math. She loved playing with her friends at lunchtime and she loved getting to wear her nice dresses to kindergarten, sometimes the satin navy one with the white bow in the middle, sometimes the velvet black one adorned with pale pink lace. She loved the juicy sausages and plump knödel her Mama made her for lunchtime. She loved the other kids, especially Wally.

Gabi met Wally on the first day of kindergarten. He sat cross-legged on the purple-speckled red rug across from the white board with the vocabulary word of the week, katze, and a small drawing of a cat's face underneath in neat black ink. His dark hair fell into his darker eyes as they scanned the pictures in the book in his lap. The rest of the kids played with wooden blocks or plastic farm animals, but Wally didn't seem to notice. Gabi couldn't say why but liked him immediately.

She sat down next to him. "What are you reading?" she asked.

He looked up. He had rather large black-rimmed glasses that made his eyes look like small dinner plates. "*Max und Moritz,*" he said. "*Eine Bubengeschichte in sieben Streichen.*"

"I love Max and Moritz," she said. *Max and Moritz: A Story of Seven Boyish Pranks* was one of the first books Mama had ever read to her. She liked the way it rhymed and she liked Max and Moritz, whom she considered some of her first friends, even if they did bad things sometimes. Gabi scooted closer, peering over Wally's shoulder.

Wally said, "Ok," and returned to his book. Beside them, Gabi's friends Otto and Samuel invaded their animal farm with the two plastic dinosaurs inexplicably packed in the toy chest with the rest.

Gabi tapped Wally on the shoulder. "Want to play with me at lunchtime?" she asked.

"Ok," he said, and returned again to his book.

.

When Eli came home that day, Gabi was already sitting at the kitchen table. He sat down across from her and stuffed a home-made roll with cheese into his mouth. "How was Kindergarten?" he asked around his roll. Despite their ten-year age gap, Gabi and her brother had always been close. All the previous year, she'd counted down the days until she could join Eli in his studies.

"Good," Gabi said, taking a small bite of the roll on her plate. "I got a boyfriend."

Eli nearly choked on his roll. "You're moving a little quick there, aren't you?" he asked. "First day and everything."

Gabi shrugged. "I don't know," she said. "His name is Wally and I love him." That was the only way Gabi knew how to describe the fluttery feeling in her chest, the burst of joy in her heart whenever she saw Wally from across the room.

Mama came into the kitchen then. She kissed Eli on the head and said, "It's true. We'll be hearing wedding bells soon."

Gabi nodded. "Maybe next week," she clarified. "We only played tag today, and then he sat next to me for story time."

Eli caught their mother's eye. Mama glanced away, grinning, and Gabi took another bite.

.

The next day, Gabi asked Wally to marry her. "We could do it on the playground," she said. "All of our friends can be there."

She had already decided that Otto could marry them, since Otto was her friend from before school. They lived on the same street and everything. Otto was the one who taught her the secret spies game, where you write notes and the first letter of every sentence spells a word. Decades later, though before she fled with little more than a suitcase full of clothing, Gabi would teach that game to her nephews.

Wally shrugged. "Sure," he said.

The next week, several of their classmates gathered around to watch Gabi and Wally on the playground. Gabi wore her lilac dress with a black headband, Wally a white shirt and slacks. Otto read from a yellow piece of craft paper, where Gabi had scratched out instructions with red crayon. She knew what he should say because Mama told her once in a bedtime story.

Otto stood in front of their friends and read, "Gabi Ruth Alt—"

"Gabriella."

Otto blinked. "Huh?"

"It has to be full names," Gabi said. "Gabriella Ruth Altenberg." Mama helped write it down and everything. All Otto had to do was read it correctly.

"Oh." Otto looked back down at the paper. "Uh, Gabriella Ruth Altenberg, do you take Wall–er–Walter David Keefer to be your husband?"

"I do," Gabi said, grinning. In her hands, she held the wildflowers from the field beyond the school gates. She'd picked them before coming to school this morning for just this occasion. Gabi knew they were there because she liked to look at them on her way home from school.

Otto turned to Wally. The sun glinted off Otto's golden hair and Wally's polished glasses. "Walter David Keefer, do you take, um, Gabriella Ruth Altenberg to be your wife?"

Wally shrugged. "I guess so," he said.

Otto threw the paper up in the air. "You're married," he said.

The other children clapped and Gabi hugged Wally. Many of the children would be there later, when Gabi got married a second time, in a synagogue many years from that moment. The yellow paper Otto had thrown caught in the breeze and landed over the fence with the wildflowers.

·

Gabi asked Mama to read her *Max und Moritz* that night. "It's the book Wally was reading when I met him," she said.

Mama pulled the book off Gabi's shelf, white and wooden. Papa had assembled it before he died, just a few months after Gabi's first birthday. Mama sat in bed beside Gabi and opened the book, full of images of Max and Moritz covered in dough or sawing the planks of their neighbor's bridge. Gabi could read now, but she usually wanted Mama to read to her at night, and besides, Max and Moritz was their special book to read together. So Mama read,

Ah, how oft we read or hear of boys we almost stand in fear of!
For example, take these stories of two youths, named Max and Moritz,
Who, instead of early turning their young minds to useful learning,
Often leered with horrid features at their lessons and their teachers.

Gabi giggled. "I like Max and Moritz," she said.

"I know, my mausi," she said.

"Why aren't there any girl Maxes and Moritzes?" she asked.

"What do you mean?"

"Like, what about Theodora and Inge?" Gabi asked. "Or Julie and Estelle?" All of those were names of girls in her class.

"Well, maybe one day you can write that story," Mama said. "Do you want me to change the names? Make Max Theodora and Moritz Inge?"

Gabi shook her head. "Just read the story, please."

Mama got back to the story and Gabi stayed awake until the sixth and very last prank, when Max and Moritz are almost baked in an oven but get away at the last minute by eating their way through the crusts they'd been trapped in. Gabi had always wondered why the title said there were seven pranks. Mama said the title must refer to pranks that hadn't happened yet.

—

Fritz's stomach couldn't handle the sea. He stood at the bow of the overcrowded ship a week before his fourteenth birthday, heaving above the choppy waves, his face ashen and his hands clammy. Eli, too, had always had a weak stomach, but Gabi tried not to think of Eli too much. She rubbed Fritz's back and murmured reassurances she thought a mother might say. "It's al right" and "I'm here" and "Everything is going to be ok." Things her mother used to say when she or Eli were ill. She did a horrible job, in her own opinion, but not once did Fritz complain.

Eventually he passed out on the deck, dehydrated. Dark eyes rolled in the back of his head, leaving only whites flecked with blood red veins. Several of the passengers stared, whispering behind their hands as though that meant Gabi couldn't see them. Wally wasn't particularly strong, but Fritz had been small even before they'd begun rationing their food, and Wally carried him back to his bed with little effort.

They spoke in low voices as Fritz slept.

"Don't be afraid," Wally told Gabi in the dark cabin. "We'll find somewhere to go. And my parents and sisters will come soon, and we can all be together." She could hardly see his face in the gloom, just a dim outline of the man she loved. The stale air trapped in the windowless room made it harder to breathe.

Gabi nodded. "I'm not afraid," she said. She was, but it wasn't as much of a lie as it could have been. She was less afraid than she'd thought she would be. It was hard to be afraid with her Wally.

Days later, Gabi spotted the Statue of Liberty before the others. The morning air was foggy, dark gray swirling overhead, but the statue's green lantern poked out between the clouds, just visible to the naked eye. The closer they got, the more of her they saw. Her massive hand holding the lantern. Her copper face greeting them to their new country.

Gabi and the others had practiced some of their English with fellow passengers, a cheerful blond couple from New Jersey who had family in Germany and spoke German somewhat well.

"You will love America," the woman said. She was under the impression that the family they'd offered to help were tourists. Gabi chose to let her believe it.

Still, when the man behind the desk at Ellis Island asked Wally for their names, he froze. *We did this one*, Gabi thought. *You know what he asked you. Your name is Walter. Walter Keefer.*

When the man asked again, Gabi stepped forward. "He is Walter Keefer," she said.

The man glanced at her, as if barely registering that she was there. "Who are you?" he asked, rather rudely in Gabi's opinion.

"I am Gabriella Keefer," she said. "Also, this is my brother. He is Fritz Altenberg." Fritz stared at a small crack in the floor and didn't say anything. Wally put an arm around his shoulders.

The man glared at Gabi and wiped his ruddy, sweaty forehead with a pink handkerchief. The sweltering room smelled even worse than the ship's cabin, of too many unwashed bodies. It whirred with the frantic movement of all those lives in transit. Gabi's ears ached with the sounds of so many overlapping languages.

He wrote something down on his form and handed it to Gabi. "Here you go," he said. "Next!"

As they left the island with nothing but their three suitcases and the clothing on their backs, a man in a suit and tie waved to them. "Welcome to America," he said.

Gabi forced a tight smile and followed Wally and Fritz back into the chilled evening air. Wally's family never would join them in the States.

.

The first person Gabi befriended in Brooklyn was Erika Neuman, who had also escaped the war from Czechoslovakia.

She was several years younger than Gabi, a cleaner with the company Gabi now worked for, and unmarried with no family. Her parents and one sister hadn't been able to join her in the States. Her English, though still broken, was better than Gabi's, and they practiced together after work.

"I am very lonely sometimes," Erika admitted to her one day back at Gabi's apartment perhaps a year after they met. Their hands were raw and chapped from cleaning supplies, as they often were. They held their fingers awkwardly, stiff from scrubbing wealthy families' toilets all week. Erika's cracked skin and bloodied knuckles didn't belong on anyone's hands, much less a girl of eighteen.

"Me too," Gabi told her. It was a horrible way to feel. She had Wally and Fritz and Erika. She wasn't alone, and yet, every time she walked down the street, not a single person looked her way in recognition. When she entered a shop, she couldn't speak with the owner for fear of her stilted English. Every time this happened, Gabi's chest would tighten and her heart would leap into her mouth, muting her entirely, even if she'd wanted to try her hand at communication. The isolation suffocated some days, held its thin fingers around her throat and squeezed.

The first year or so, Otto had sent her the occasional letter, telling her that since joining the SS, he'd managed to get Samuel and several others from their class out of Germany. Arye and his family. Marcel and his wife. Frank and his parents. He'd stopped sending letters a few years ago, though. Gabi considered reaching out to his parents. Then she decided she'd rather not know what happened to him.

Gabi would have been friends with Erika back in Germany, probably. Perhaps if they had met at school or they went to the same temple. Either way, it didn't really matter. Erika was all she had here and it wouldn't do for Gabi to fabricate the origins of their relationship. They stayed wonderful friends through the years and Erika was one of the first Gabi told about her pregnancy, besides Wally and Fritz. Like Wally, Erika beamed at her and gasped. "Congratulations," she cried. "I am really happy for you."

Gabi accepted the tea Erika held out to her in a glass mug, one of two that Erika owned. "Thank you for saying to me," Erika added. "I want to know."

"Of course," Gabi said. Erika was twenty-four now to Gabi's thirty. In the six years they'd been in the States, Erika had never dated.

Erika was in the delivery room months later, with Wally and Fritz, as Gabi suffered contractions, each longer and deeper than the last. Gabi gasped and held onto Wally's hand as another tore through her.

"Scheiße," she swore in German. Beside them, Fritz translated for Erika. Fritz's English was the best of all of them. He'd turned nineteen not long ago, but to Gabi, it felt like he had been an adult for much longer.

The midwife at her feet looked up at her. "Gabriella, hon, I need you to push hard."

"What does she think I'm doing?" Gabi whispered in German to Wally, but she pushed harder all the same. She screamed as her child squeezed its way into the world, soon to be separate from her.

"It's a girl," the midwife said and all of a sudden the tension in Gabi's body released. Her insides unfurled in a way that was half-nauseating, half-relieving. From what felt like a long way away, she heard a baby scream.

"Oh," she said. She sat up, Fritz's hand on her sweat-soaked back for support. Wally cut the umbilical cord and took their baby girl in his arms. Tears ran down his face as he handed her to Gabi, and Gabi realized she was crying too. She hadn't cried since her first year in the States.

"What is her name?" Erika asked.

Gabi looked up at Wally, and Wally said, "Rebecca." For Gabi's mother, Ruth, and Wally's youngest sister, Rachel.

"She's beautiful," Fritz said, and Gabi squeezed his hand.

"She's your cousin," Gabi said.

"She's my niece now," Fritz said with a small, sad smile. Gabi frowned and looked down at her daughter. Rebecca's large brown eyes, Wally's eyes, squinted up at her and she squirmed in Gabi's arms.

Gabi looked back at Fritz. In so many ways, he resembled his father. They shared the same dark curls, the same bright eyes and wide nose. But in all the ways that counted, he was so different. He was so reserved compared to Eli, who had always made friends easily. He was compassionate, yes, but in a quiet way. He was pragmatic, not a dreamer. Gabi loved Fritz endlessly, but he was not the uncle her daughter should have had.

In German, Gabi said to Fritz, "If she had been born back home, she would have been your cousin."

—

The year Gabi birthed Rebecca was the same year she started collecting twist-ties. Blue and red and yellow, from whatever prepackaged food they came on, all stuffed in the top kitchen drawer, wall-papered with red poppies by some previous occupant.

She and Wally were always careful to save. They'd had to ration their food before they left Germany. When they first got to America, they had no money. Even now, they had to pace themselves throughout the week to have enough food for the four of them, even with Fritz, who made the most money as a secretary. Twist-ties weren't food, though, and Wally didn't seem to understand, no matter how many times they argued about it.

"You don't need them," Wally said, but still, he never discarded her stores.

"We could," Gabi said. "What if we need them one day and we've just thrown them away?" She collected other things too. Dead batteries each time she changed them. Bottle caps from her own drinks, from the drinks her loved ones chucked in the trash before Gabi fished them out again. Bags from the grocery store, both paper and plastic. The bags they did use, sometimes, but she always had more. They never used the bottle caps, nor the batteries, nor the twist ties, but she kept them nonetheless.

.

It wasn't long before Gabi became pregnant again. Rebecca was two and Gabi was happy to have her children so close in age. Still, her dream of having a house full of kids for her and Wally felt like another life. Now, she wouldn't be able to afford so many children, even if she did want them. She and Wally would have to be more careful.

She meant to tell Erika at work that day, but Erika never showed up to Mrs. Hanlon's house, much to the older woman's displeasure. Mrs. Hanlon muttered something about ungrateful immigrants and stomped off. Not once did she look at Gabi or thank her for doing such a thorough job by herself.

After work, Gabi went to Erika's and knocked gently on the door to avoid bruising her already raw hands. She waited a minute before she knocked again, but still, no one answered. Gabi tried the knob and found the door unlocked. She slipped inside and called, "Erika?" Still no answer.

Erika's apartment was smaller than Gabi and Wally's, so it didn't take long to search. She found Erika hanging in the closet, a thick rope around her slender neck, her eyes bulging and her cheeks purple. She left no note.

Later, when Gabi had calmed down enough to tell Wally, he held her so his shirt muffled her cries.

"Erika must have been so lonely," he said, "to do such a thing."

Gabi thought back to their conversations, so many of them, that proved Wally right, but she protested that they were Erika's family now, and how could she leave her niece behind?

How could she leave me?

———

The second time Gabi married Wally, they were eighteen years old, Gabi nearly nineteen. The ceremony took place not on the playground, but at the synagogue they had attended for years. Otto did not marry them, though he was there, wearing a black tux and standing beside Wally, the latter of whom was telling anyone who would listen that he was the luckiest man in the world.

Gabi's cousin Brigitte tucked a final pale pink and still blooming flower in Gabi's hair in front of the ornate, gold-rimmed mirror. Gabi's hair fell to her shoulder blades in waves and her cheeks were flushed with rouge. "Do you think he'll like the dress?" Gabi asked Brigitte.

Brigitte's sister Manya laughed and said, "Who wouldn't?"

Even though Gabi's cousins had grown up between Germany and France, their German was flawless. Much better than Gabi's French, which was very nearly nonexistent. Her father had been French and Eli claimed he used to speak to them in the language, but Gabi couldn't remember much of her father, even in German. He must have done, though, because Eli spoke French nearly as well as the cousins spoke German.

Gabi had thought of her father often over the past few weeks. She thought of all the ones who couldn't be there. Papa, of course, who died not long after Gabi was born. Her grandparents, long passed on her mother's side and too frail to travel from France on her father's. The Rosenbaums, her neighbors and family friends who moved years ago to America, when Mr. Rosenbaum's business had begun to lose customers. His daughter, Goldie, was the girl everyone thought Eli would marry until the family fled.

"You look stunning, my mausi," Mama said, interrupting Gabi's reverie. The dress had been Mama's, long ago. The shoulders and the skirt poofed slightly and the top was adorned with carefully placed lace. Mama's own grandmother had made it when she married.

Gabi looked up at Mama, grinning. "I'm getting married today."

"Yes," Mama said. "And for real this time." Mama tucked a hair behind Gabi's ear and stood back. Her voice wavered and she said, "You won't be mine anymore."

Gabi stood up and hugged Mama tight, standing slightly crooked, the best she could in her dress. This was the woman who raised her, the woman who never once made fun of her for her childhood crush. "I'll always be yours," Gabi said. Mama's eyes sparkled with unshed tears, but she didn't cry. Mama never cried. Instead, she offered her arm and lead Gabi to the door.

Brigitte left to take her place at the front of the temple as Gabi's maid of honor. Manya gave Gabi a quick kiss on the cheek before and left as well, to sit with Eli, his wife Susan, and their two boys, then seven and three. Wally's father stepped behind the door to the back of the synagogue and held his hand out to Gabi. "Shall we?" he asked.

Gabi took his hand and gave it a squeeze. "Thank you," she said, and Wally's father squeezed her hand in return.

Wally brightened as soon as he spotted Gabi from down the aisle. He gave her a small wave and she returned it, beaming at their family and friends as she walked. The cantor sang in soothing baritones. When she and Mr. Keefer reached Wally, Mr. Keefer gave him a quick hug and sat down. Wally winked at Gabi from behind his glasses, black as always and oval-rimmed, which he had gotten just for the occasion.

Rabbi Isaac, a balding man with wire-rimmed, square-framed glasses and a gap between his two front teeth just a little wider than Gabi's, smiled at them both and recited a prayer. They'd both known Rabbi Isaac from the time they were children, since he had walked up to them at temple and jokingly asked why they hadn't had their wedding (the first one) at synagogue.

Gabi's mind wandered briefly onto the life she would have with Wally. They would live close to her heart, her Mama and Eli, and she could see her nephews every day. They would have kids of their own, half a dozen of them. Children with Gabi's dark eyes and Wally's long nose, or else Gabi's nearly black hair and Wally's narrow chin, and Fritz and Albert would watch them when Gabi and Wally spent the evening at Eli and Susan's place. Together, she and Wally would buy a house and plant a garden with all sorts of flowers. Perhaps Gabi would learn how to grow her own food there.

"Do you, Gabriella Ruth Altenberg, take Walter David Keefer to be your lawfully wedded husband, in sickness and in health, as long as you both shall live?"

Gabi glanced at Otto, who was grinning sheepishly, perhaps remembering the kindergarten wedding he'd officiated so long ago. She turned her gaze back to Wally and said, "I do."

"And do you, Walter David Keefer, take Gabriella Ruth Altenberg to be your lawfully wedded wife, in sickness and in health, for as long as you both shall live?"

Wally grabbed Gabi's hand, even though he wasn't supposed to yet, and said, "I do."

"I now pronounce you husband and wife," Rabbi Isaac said, grinning. "You may now kiss the bride."

Wally crushed the glass beneath his feet and pulled Gabi forward by the hand. They kissed and their family and friends cheered, "Mazel tov!" In the first row, Fritz leaned forward and asked Eli a question Gabi couldn't hear. Susan would later tell her he asked if this meant Fritz and Albert would have cousins soon.

.

Gabi danced for hours in her mother's and grandmother's and great-grandmother's dress. With Wally, first, and then with Eli and Otto and her cousins and nephews. Mama sat with Wally's mother and father at one of the circular, covered tables surrounding the dance floor. The flowers Gabi wanted for her future garden sat as centerpieces in golden vases.

Wally's three sisters danced with Fritz and Albert until Albert was too tired to dance anymore. Wally's youngest sister was only older than Fritz by three years, but she was thrilled to be dancing with the "babies." "They're adorable," Rachel cooed to Susan, who had Albert half-sleeping in her arms. "I want one." Wally's mother laughed.

The party was over sooner than either of them would have liked, and not soon enough, either. Gabi left the wedding a Keefer and her new sisters-in-law all hugged her tight and welcomed her to the family. Wally's parents, the other Mr. and Mrs. Keefer, had to usher the girls away so that the couple could leave. Wally's older sister Bettina cried the whole time, her own husband on her arm.

They made it to Mama's house, where they would live until they bought a home of their own (Mama would stay with Eli for the night). They tumbled into Gabi's twin bed together and spent the rest of the evening in each other's arms, joking about how the first thing they had to do was get a bigger bed, but neither of them really minded. Gabi expected a rush of pain that came with her first time, but she couldn't suppress a gasp at the sharp ache below her belly.

Wally paused. "Are you all right?"

Gabi nodded. She shifted slightly, her hands on Wally's shoulders. "Don't stop," she insisted.

Near midnight, long after the ache had lessened, Wally gathered Gabi in his arms and said, "I love you."

Gabi rolled over so that she faced Wally. "I love you too," she said, touching his face. She fell asleep like that, tucked into Wally so that her head was just under his chin and their legs criss-crossed under the covers. For the night, she lived under the delusion that nothing could hurt her so long as she had Wally, so long as she was happy.

The delusion lasted six years, through more and more friends leaving, just like the Rosenbaums. Through yellow fabric stars and the realization that Germany, a country of which she was no longer a citizen, didn't care whether she lived or died. It lasted until she lost the only man she'd loved for longer than she'd loved her Wally.

—

They didn't often frequent the secondhand bookstore by their Brooklyn home, so Gabi thought it fate when she found a battered, German copy of *Max und Moritz* on the shelf closest to the ground, nestled between a peeling Agatha Christie paperback and a hardcover *Gone With The Wind* without the dust jacket. She blinked back tears and ran her finger over the faded cover art. Max on the left, his dark hair puffing out on his round head, and Moritz beside him, a small smile creating dimples on his pink cheeks. Gabi tucked the book under her arm, made the purchase, and rushed home to tell Wally. "It was the book you were reading when we met," she told him.

Wally laughed. "I'd almost forgotten," he said. "I was mostly looking at the pictures."

They were doing a bit better, financially. Wally's friend from Berlin had started a business with his American cousins and brought Wally on board. Gabi needn't have bought such a worn-out copy, but she liked the idea that someone else had read the book before her. Perhaps even someone from home.

"Will you read it to the girls?" he asked. Rebecca, now five, adored her younger sister, Eliana, but hadn't quite been able to say her name when she had been born. They called her El, then Ellie. They'd named her for Eli and Erika.

"Rebecca, maybe," she said. "The last story gets a bit scary."

"We were both reading those books when we were Ellie's age," Wally said. "She's so smart she could probably read it herself by now."

Gabi shrugged. "Still."

She opened the book that night, tracing her hand over the illustrations of Max and Moritz. Old friends. She had left so many behind. Gabi reveled in the familiar rhymes, heard Mama's familiar and careful cadence in her head as she read the story.

Gabi got to the last story, the one where Max and Moritz eat their way out of bread crusts before they get baked alive, and frowned. There were still several pages left in the book.

She turned to a seventh story. Max and Moritz bothered another innocent townsman. A farmer. She turned the page and read on, her frown becoming more pronounced with every previously unread word. Her fictional friends wandered onto the farmer's land, intending mischief. The farmer had other ideas, fed them to the grinder, and then fed the resulting product to the ducks. No one mourned Max and Moritz. In fact, the townsfolk rejoiced.

Gabi closed the book, her mouth open and her heart hammering. She thought back, but she could never remember reading the book herself. Mama had always read it to her.

Mama said the seventh story must be one that hadn't happened yet...

Wally poked his head in. "I thought tomorrow we could—Are you all right?"

Gabi wiped a tear from her eye and shrugged. "Yes. It's silly."

Wally sat beside her in their bed. "Max and Moritz?"

"I didn't know," she said. "That they died in the end."

Wally looked down at the book once more, and then up at her. "But you said, the last story..."

"The one where they're almost baked in an oven," Gabi said. "But they survive. It turns out they don't, really."

Wally put a gentle hand on her arm. "I'm sorry," he said.

Gabi shrugged and put the book on her bedside table. "It's silly," she said again. "I don't know why I'm behaving this way." The next morning, she put the book in her closet. She never read it to the girls.

.

Kindergarten was called the same thing in America, funnily enough. That fall, Gabi walked Rebecca to the school called Jewish Community Center down the street. She held Rebecca's small, warm hand tightly in her own.

"I'm excited to make friends," Rebecca said in English, the only language she knew fluently. She wore a pale pink dress with a red sash. It wasn't one of Gabi's, from before. Gabi had left all of those dresses in Berlin when she fled. Besides, young Gabi wouldn't have chosen that color pink. It was far too muted.

"Uncle Fredrick will be there to get you after school." They'd decided to call Fritz Fredrick around the girls. He already had so many people ask him to repeat his name when he told them, so many people ask him where on earth a name like that came from. His English was so good, besides, that he could very nearly pass for American with the name Fredrick but for a light accent. At work, they called him Fred.

Inside, Gabi asked the secretary in careful English how to get to the classroom. There, a young woman, younger than Gabi, greeted Rebecca with a smile and a hug. "Welcome to kindergarten! Let me show you your desk."

"Ok!" Rebecca followed this strange woman inside, to a desk with Rebecca's name written in loopy letters at the top. Several parents milled about the classroom, but there were far more children. Tiny, multicolored chairs sat tucked under each desk. Had Gabi's kindergarten classroom also smelled this way, like glue and crayons and craft paper? Had she ever been small enough that she could have fit into one of those chairs? She couldn't remember now, three decades removed from the day she met her Wally.

Rebecca saw the books and ran over to pull one off a small wooden shelf. The rug was patterned with the English alphabet, each letter surrounded by a different color block.

"She seems excited," the teacher said. "You're welcome to chat with the parents for a bit, but I'm going to have to ask you all to leave in ten minutes or so."

"All right," Gabi said, even though she didn't know what the word "chat" meant. Talk? Mill about?

She glanced over at the parents. They all seemed to know each other, or at least speak the same language. Gabi looked back to Rebecca, who was already speaking with two little girls, both with blonde hair. Gabi turned and left the classroom.

.

With Ellie asleep in her room, Gabi sat on her and Wally's bed and stared at a discolored spot on the wall. She had no jobs today. She'd been taking less of them with the kids, especially after she gave birth to Ellie. Gabi glanced down to her left, as though expecting to see Rebecca beside her, but of course she wasn't. Rebecca was at school, excited in a way Gabi hadn't been since she left Germany.

Gabi slipped into Ellie and Rebecca's room and hovered over Ellie's sleeping form. Her daughter's dark hair fanned out behind her head on her Winnie-the-Pooh pillow. Her arms stuck out from under the quilt Gabi had finished just last year, squares haphazardly stitched together to create a memory for her daughters. She ran her finger over Ellie's cheek, turned around, and left.

Chapter Two: Will and Won't
1995-2006

In hindsight, Jason could pinpoint the exact moment Grandma Rebecca decided to die. He could see her living room (their living room) in his mind's eye. He saw the cream-colored couch where he and his mom sat, his mom closer to the door, just in case she needed to make a sudden escape, as she so often did. He saw the dark burgundy walls, redone several years ago in a color Grandma loved and Jason's mom detested. Grandma Rebecca said the latter didn't matter anymore, since Lena and her loser of a boyfriend (Jason's words, not Grandma's) didn't live with them anyway.

He saw the photos, all so vivid in his head from so many years of studying them. The photo just above where Jason sat depicted Grandma Rebecca and Grandpa Silas on their wedding day, both of them smiling brightly at the camera, their faces stark in black and white film. Grandma Rebecca's dark hair curled out from under her lace veil on either side of her heart-shaped face. Grandpa Silas had one arm around Grandma's shoulders, the other around her waist. Jason had never met Grandpa Silas, but he recognized his features in his mother and Aunt Claire, namely the deep blue eyes they all shared.

Beside that photo, his great-grandparents Gabi and Wally sat frozen in their Brooklyn home years ago, each with a close-lipped smile and tired eyes. They were in their fifties or early sixties here, not many years before Wally's death. Like with his grandfather, Jason had never met Wally, but his great-grandmother had been a fixture of his childhood, quiet and distant but present. He visited often when he stayed with Grandma Rebecca over his mother's long stints in and out of rehab. By the time he moved in with Grandma Rebecca for good, his great-grandmother had been dead a year.

The photo of his mother and Aunt Claire sat above this one, depicting the women as children in matching pink dresses with overlarge bows. Lena must have been five or six, Aunt Claire three or four. They could have been twins but for the age difference, both with striking eyes and high cheekbones that, much later in her life, would become even more pronounced when Lena overdid it on the pills and lost too much weight. In the photo, Lena held her sister's hand. Aunt Claire smiled up at Lena. Lena didn't smile at all.

Last, beside the photo of his mother and above the photo of his grandmother, was a photo of Jason at his eighth birthday party, blowing out the candles on a thickly-iced chocolate cake Grandma Rebecca had made just for him. His great grand-mother's hand hovered in the background, ready in case Jason needed help or he accidentally started a fire with the candles. Grandma Rebecca had taken that one, counting down patiently so Jason could know when to make a wish. Jason was the only brown person in the photos.

"If you didn't get the scholarship, no dice," Jason's mom said in the moments before the realization. Lena stretched her left leg over two of the three couch cushions. She always did this when she visited, took over the place like she owned it, even though she refused all of Grandma Rebecca's offers throughout Jason's childhood to move back in. Jason sat on the other cushion, as close as he could be to the arm of the couch without sitting on it instead.

"I could work, though," Jason said. "And I'll pay you back." Lena didn't have much money (these days, she spent anything she had to spare on getting high), but Jason thought maybe she would give him what she had. He should have learned by now not to hope when it came to his mother and her addiction.

"Why don't you ask your rich dad?" Lena asked. "Or your grandma?"

"Sid isn't rich," Jason said, but Lena ignored him and yelled, "Hey, Mom!"

Grandma Rebecca poked her head around the corner and said, "You rang?"

Just as Lena and Aunt Claire were so alike in physicality, they were their mother's clones. They had the same sloping noses, the same thick eyebrows. Even Lena's blue eyes were shaped the same as Grandma Rebecca's, heavy lidded with thick eyelashes. Grandma Rebecca's graying hair was down to her thin shoulders, but it used to be exactly Lena's shade. Lena had tied her still-dark hair back in a messy ponytail and several strands had escaped, placing themselves carelessly around her face.

"You want to pay for Jason's college, since you've decided you make a better mother than me anyway?"

"Leave it alone," Jason whispered.

Lena laughed, mirthless. "What, it's okay to ask me for money, but not her?" She gestured to Grandma Rebecca, who had her arms crossed.

"She's already helping me," Jason said.

"Whatever. You coming over for dinner tomorrow?"

Jason shrugged and Lena rolled her eyes. "Fancy college boy is too good for his mother," she said, standing. "You know, I never graduated college. Grandma Rebecca never went to college." She picked up her coat now, which she had left lying on the floor by the door when she came in. "Waste of money," she said. "Waste of time." She left, slamming the door behind her.

"I'm sorry," Jason said, readjusting himself so that he was sitting on more of the couch cushion.

"Don't be sorry," Grandma Rebecca said. "She's my daughter, you know. I'm used to it."

"Really, you don't have to help me anymore," Jason said. Grandma didn't like to talk about it, but Jason had read between the lines over the last few years. Heart problems ("I'm not even sixty yet!") meant expensive medication. Lena said she was probably making them up to get out of helping her grandson. Jason wanted to scream in her face whenever she said that.

"Hmm." Grandma Rebecca frowned. When Jason replayed the scene in his mind, now that he knew what came next, he could see the gears turning in Grandma's brain, calculating the cost of her own life against Jason's future.

———

Before he met Sid, Grandma Rebecca was the closest thing he had to a parent. A real parent, not someone who did drugs in the living room with their boyfriend after work and forgot to take their son to get his braces off for three weeks. Jason moved out when he was twelve years old and Lena had never once asked him to move back. Grandma Rebecca called to get Jason's braces off not long after that.

Sid was Jason's real father. Not Rich, who came into their lives when Jason was ten and who sometimes hit him when he thought Jason was getting too uptight for his own good. Rich poked fun at him for being Indian. Rich said he smelled like curry. Rich made fun of him for being Jewish, even though Lena was too. "You don't look Jewish," he would say, or, "Why don't you wear those little hats?" Then he would laugh, like he'd just made the funniest joke in the world. When Rich made an ass of himself like that, Jason and Lena would sometimes lock eyes and for a moment, Jason could almost feel bad for her. Almost.

Grandma Rebecca called him "Dick" behind his back. "It's a real nickname for Richard," she would say, winking at Jason. Sometimes Jason would smile at that. Other times, Jason would shrug and pretend Rich didn't bother him, even though Jason could hear the slurs Rich hurled at him in his dreams, feel the sting of Rich's backhand as he laid his cheek against the pillow. Rich was probably the reason Lena relapsed the year they met.

Jason didn't even meet Sid until he was thirteen, and only then because Grandma Rebecca reached out on Jason's behalf.

"Of course I'll always be there for you," she said. "But it can't hurt to get to know him too."

He still didn't know how Grandma had tracked Sid down in the first place.

Sid lived in Manhattan, on the Upper East Side. He drove down to Long Island the week after Grandma called and took Jason out to lunch at Jason's favorite diner, the one Grandma Rebecca took him to for special occasions, like birthdays or end-of-school celebrations. He showed Jason photos of his wife, Chawla; their son, Ryan; and their daughter, Molly. Sid hadn't even known Jason existed until Grandma Rebecca got in touch.

"But I'm glad she did," Sid said.

"Yeah," Jason said. Sid and Jason looked nearly as similar as Grandma Rebecca and Lena did to each other. They had the same coarse, black hair and the same crooked smile. Sid's beard concealed the lower part of his face, but Jason guessed they would have had the same dimples in their cheeks.

They sat across from each other in plastic green booths. Jason and Grandma knew the diner owners from temple, a woman called Esther and her husband, Jacob, both of whom were around Grandma's age, maybe a bit older. Jason ordered first and got blueberry pancakes. Sid got chocolate chip with a side of mixed fruit.

"You can come see us any time you like," Sid said.

"Ok," Jason said, even though he knew Grandma Rebecca would probably be too busy with work to drive him all the way to Manhattan. Briefly, he wondered what he'd say if Esther or Jacob walked in, what he would tell them about the strange man sitting across from him, but he didn't have to worry. Jason didn't see anyone he knew.

—

Even before Jason moved in with Grandma Rebecca, his favorite childhood memories involved spending time with her. She would take him to Beth Shalom on the weekends and holidays. Even years later, Jason could recall with perfect clarity the vividness of the Purim decorations, the masks the younger children colored and hung up on the walls of the temple. He could taste sweet tang of apples and honey on his tongue during Rosh Hashanah solely by remembering.

During Sukkot, Grandma Rebecca would hoist Jason onto her broad shoulders and let him decorate the top of the Sukkah with the adults, threading long strands of multi-colored paper through the beams that connected the walls. Because his grandmother was so young, the other kids would often assume she was his mother. Jason never bothered correcting them. Neither had Grandma Rebecca.

Without Grandma Rebecca though, temple wasn't nearly as fun. He was the only brown kid in his Hebrew School class and he pretended not to notice when the other kids whispered to their neighbors and pointed under their desks. Jason stopped going to Hebrew School after his Bar Mitzvah and only went to temple with Grandma Rebecca after that. She asked him repeatedly if he would reconsider. He never told her the real reason he'd stopped.

His Bar Mitzvah was an affair in and of itself, not that much happened at the service. Jason, just on the thin line between preteen and teenage, managed to keep his voice from cracking more than twice while reciting carefully memorized prayers. They had a small reception at the temple after with just thirty guests, nearly twenty of them his own age, plus the temple staff and his grandma's cousin, Zane, who came with his children. The other parties he'd gone to that year were much larger.

This was several months before Jason met Sid, before he learned of his half-siblings. His only immediate family was Grandma Rebecca and Lena, the latter of whom never showed up, not that he expected her to do so. He brought it up (casually, he hoped) on her last visit to Grandma's, when she came by still slightly tipsy from whatever she'd had to drink the night before, or maybe even that day, even though it was barely noon. "Are you coming?" he asked. He had been living with Grandma Rebecca for three months by then.

Lena sobered immediately. "I don't know," she said. A steel edge in her voice made Jason flinch.

Grandma Rebecca sat up straighter. "You won't come to your own son's Bar Mitzvah?"

Lena sighed. "I don't know, Mom. The last time I went to temple was a little traumatic." Grandma Rebecca frowned, and Lena leaned forward slightly. "Claire's Bat Mitzvah," she said. "Remember?"

"I remember," Grandma said, still frowning in confusion. "It was lovely."

"God, I can't." Lena stood. "I need rent money." Grandma Rebecca's frown deepened, but she reached into her purse and handed Lena several bills. They didn't see Lena again until after the ceremony.

Theoretically, his mom had been sober for the first three or so years of Jason's life, but he couldn't remember it. The first time she went to a detox program, Jason had been six. Before then, Grandma Rebecca had pleaded with her. She cried more than once, even before the worst of it, and Jason had never forgotten the pained lines of her worried face. They still haunted his dreams.

In the two years before the program, when she was in the worst of it, Lena avoided Grandma Rebecca and the rest of their family almost entirely, except when she needed money. She used to bring Jason with her and held a finger to her lips when he caught her sneaking a few twenties at a time from Grandma Rebecca's wallet. When Jason, age five, told his grandmother in a fit of guilt, she told him she knew. "I don't know how to help her," she said.

Lena got sober (for the moment) and that was the one time she and Jason stayed at Grandma Rebecca's, when they couldn't afford to keep their own apartment. Lena slept in her old room while Jason took his Aunt Claire's old room, the one that would later become his own. More than once, Jason caught his mom crying when she thought no one was listening. He never checked in on her, never let her know he heard. When he saw her the next day, her face would have always fallen back into that stoic mask he'd grown up with, the one he'd learned to love and loathe in equal measure.

—

Grandma Rebecca's favorite saying come SAT season was, "You'll never know unless you try," even though, "I'd be fine with community college. Really."

"If you go to community college, you go to community college," Grandma Rebecca said one night over dinner. Her specialty, grilled cheese and tomato soup. "But you should know what your options are before you pick between them."

"Ok."

Grandma Rebecca squeezed his hand gently. "I'll be proud of you no matter what," she said, and Jason believed her in a way he never would have believed Lena. Grandma Rebecca never lied to him.

He studied everywhere. At lunch in the cafeteria, surrounded by elated voices taking their mid-day breaks from schoolwork. Under the desk during class, which he got in trouble for more than once. In Grandma Rebecca's office in front of the grainy photo she kept of Grandpa Silas, grinning on a sandy beach in Jamaica, a trip they'd taken when Lena and Aunt Claire were twelve and ten.

Jason's scores ended up being the highest in his class. "I knew it," Grandma Rebecca said when he told her. She held him tight, and he breathed in the scent of her. Joy and peppermint and sweat. She let go and beamed at him, and Jason knew that as long as he made his grandmother happy, he was doing all right.

.

Lena came by sometimes at night, when she thought Jason would be sleeping. Sometimes she pretended it wasn't for money. Most of the time she didn't.

Jason heard Grandma Rebecca tell Lena about the SAT late one night. She thought Jason might even be able to apply to Duke or Stanford. In spite of himself, Jason's heart filled with pride. He *could* go to Duke if he wanted. He believed, for a moment, that he had a future. Until, that was, Lena laughed.

"He might get in," she said, "but he can't go."

"Sure he can."

"With what money?" Jason pictured them in the living room down the hall from his room. Grandma Rebecca would be sitting on the chair beside the couch, perhaps. Lena would be standing over her, her hands shaking slightly like they did when she was jonesing, which was most of the time when she deigned to visit.

"We can take out a loan."

Jason imagined his mother smiling here. A cold smile, one that left her eyes flat. He was very familiar with that smile. He got it almost every time he asked for something. "With what credit?" she asked.

"Scholarships. Work study."

"He's gotta earn those."

"We'll find a way," Grandma Rebecca said.

They spoke for a little while longer, and for the first time in the four years since Jason moved in with Grandma Rebecca,

Lena left empty-handed. He listened to his grandmother tread quietly down the hall to use the bathroom. He fell asleep while she was still brushing her teeth.

.

Soon after he was denied a few too many scholarships, nearly a year after his SATs, Jason swallowed his pride and asked Sid for money. "It could be a loan," he said. "And I would pay you back."

Jason had visited several times over the last year. Mostly, he took the train by himself, but he had come up with Grandma Rebecca for Christmas the month before. They brought a toy robot for Ryan, now eleven, and a small puzzle with an array of multicolored birds on it for Molly, now eight. Sid and Chawla had put a small menorah, borrowed from a neighbor, in the window for Jason and Grandma. They never did end up lighting it.

Now, seated across from each other in Sid's living room, Sid smiled down at Jason, but like Jason frequently saw with Lena, the smile didn't quite reach Sid's eyes. In this case, though, Jason saw sadness rather than annoyance or outright dislike. It was a welcome change, even though Sid spoke the exact words he'd been dreading.

"I wish I could," Sid said.

Jason looked past him, at the Christmas tree still in the corner. It was a fake tree. Plastic. "Never mind, then."

"No, I really want to," Sid said. "I want to. It's just that Chawla's business isn't doing well, and—"

"No, I get it," Jason said, picking at a thread on his sleeve. "It's fine." He probably had to think about college for Molly and Ryan too.

Jason heard thumping on the stairs and Molly dashed into the living room, out of breath. "Oh, hi Jason. Dad, can I have ice cream?"

"We just had lunch, Mol."

"Yeah, but ice cream is, like, a different section of your stomach."

"Later," Sid said. "For dessert."

Molly rolled her eyes. "Whatever. Jason, do you want to play with me?"

"Sure," Jason said. As strange as he still felt around Sid, Jason loved Molly and Ryan. They didn't understand the concept of "half-siblings" yet, nor did they question how abruptly Jason had come into their lives. Ryan was thrilled to have a brother, Molly a playmate. They went up to Molly's room, painted sky blue with the occasional bird done by Sid's careful hand.

More than once, Jason wondered what it would have been like growing up with Sid. Would he have painted Jason's room like he painted Molly's? Would he have bought Jason puzzles with his favorite characters or recent interests? Jason would have gladly exchanged all the ice cream in the world for a parent who cared.

Yet another new puzzle lay nearly completed on the floor beside her unmade bed. Molly gazed up at Jason with the wide eyes she shared with her mom. Not Sid's eyes, nor Jason's.

"Could you help me finish?" she asked, pointing to the puzzle. "I just have a few pieces left, but they're all green like the leaves."

"Sure," Jason said. He got on his knees beside Molly and examined the box. The photo on the front showed the puzzle completed, a Central Park picnic with a group of blonde tourists on a checkered blanket. Together, Jason and Molly stuck piece after piece into the puzzle until something stayed.

—

The day Grandma Rebecca's doctor told them—in the clinical, unaffected tone that doctors so often used—that Grandma had a heart condition, Jason cried for hours. He was fifteen and far too old for such a raw display of emotion, but he hid himself up in his room and sobbed nonetheless. He even tried praying, although he didn't know which prayer to say to keep his grandmother well, nor did he know to whom exactly he was praying.

At dinner that night, he feigned calm and listened as Grandma Rebecca told him all about her sister.

"She had the same thing," Grandma Rebecca said, "but she had it from the time we were children."

Grandma Rebecca rarely spoke about her sister. She didn't have any photos in the house, though there were a few in the old family photo albums she kept in the closet in her room. Eliana. Ellie.

"Is that how she died?" Jason asked quietly, between bites of mashed potato. He wasn't particularly hungry, but he didn't want Grandma Rebecca to worry about him too.

"Yes," she said. "I still think about her all the time."

In Jason's dream that night, he hovered outside a hospital room in a long, tiled hallway while doctors poked at Grandma Rebecca's ice-white body. He felt the cool of her fingers, even though they weren't touching. Jason didn't touch anything in the dream, but he felt it all anyway. The cold metal of the silver carts along the hallway. The ache of the little girl in the room across from Grandma's whose leg had just been bound in a cast.

No one told him, but there was a break in the dream and he knew Grandma Rebecca was dead. He fell to the floor in agony (he was in the hospital room suddenly) and his whole body burned with grief. He forgot how to breathe in solidarity.

In the morning, Jason woke screaming.

He did his best to forget the dream, but it seemed more real to him than the very much alive Grandma Rebecca somehow making him oatmeal, blueberries and all, before school. He looked around and realized the whole house recalled their life together. The pictures of them on the walls. Grandma Rebecca's knitted blue blanket on the couch. Were she to die tomorrow, her presence would cling to this place like a leech.

Jason began to read ghost stories. In one of his favorites, a girl called Lauren tried to ignore the ghost of her cousin running around her aunt and uncle's house, but it became increasingly difficult. The sprightly Danielle had always liked attention, even as a ghost. In life, she staged major productions in the backyard, with rows of chairs for all her friends and neighbors, who applauded for the small group of pre-teens on the stage that was Danielle's back porch.

Since Lauren was two years older, Danielle always made her play the adults. Ms. Hannigan in *Annie*. The nuns in *The Sound of Music*. Even when Lauren asked to play other parts, Danielle would impatiently explain her logic. Lauren's younger sister was Danielle's age and therefore got the roles Lauren often coveted, even if her sister was sometimes made to play boys.

As the story started, Lauren was fifty-two to Danielle's forever fourteen. Lauren sat next to her mother, across from her aunt and uncle, and ignored Danielle making faces at her from behind her parents' backs. Lauren took a sip of her tea and had to ask her uncle twice to repeat the question she failed to hear in the face of his daughter's distraction.

Danielle was the first ghost Lauren ever saw, though she saw several in the intervening years. There's the old man in the drugstore with the coveralls and the white mustache that consistently asked her about her day. The dark-haired woman on the street corner who carried a woven basket and asked Lauren for change when she passed. Lauren learned to identify them by their sheen, the shimmer that seemed to radiate from their skin. In the end, Lauren freed Danielle's ghost from her former home, allowing her to pass to the other side.

The story comforted Jason. He liked the idea of a living woman so intertwined with the afterlife she could commune with ghosts. He liked the idea of an afterlife at all.

In the three or so years since Grandma Rebecca's diagnosis, Jason thought about her heart condition less and less. The doctor promised on more than one occasion that as long as she took her meds and remained otherwise healthy, Grandma Rebecca, "should outlive us all."

Jason certainly hadn't expected to find Grandma Rebecca dead one morning in April, a week after he turned eighteen. She was lying in bed, on her back like a stranded crab. Her left hand dangled over the edge of the mattress. The other stayed hidden, tucked under the blankets. In the six years Jason had lived with his Grandma, she'd never slept in on a school day. Her lack of presence in the kitchen that morning had prompted Jason to look for her in the first place.

"Grandma?" He shook her shoulder and her head flopped against the pillow, her graying hair slipping down over her eyes. "Grandma Rebecca!" Jason put his head to her chest and heard nothing.

Jason took a deep breath. Then another. He screwed his eyes shut tight and whispered, "I'm sorry." He tucked her left hand back under the sheets (she got cold easily). Then he made his own sandwich, grabbed his book bag, and left for school.

Jason insisted on paying rent at Sid's place from his after-school job as the cashier at the hardware store, even though Sid and Chawla both said several times that it wasn't necessary. He shared a room with Ryan, who protested at first ("I don't *want* to share my room!"), but a week later only grumbled incoher-ently when Jason wouldn't play bots with him.

Lena turned up that first week, her usually wild hair combed back and braided. She wore a pale pink blouse, one Jason had never seen before. Sid had answered the door and Jason found them at Sid and Chawla's kitchen table, both of them sitting straight up, like a pair of Ryan's robots. Jason looked back and forth between them and wondered how two such people could have gotten together in the first place. The thought had never crossed his mind before, or else he'd squashed it before it could. He didn't care to think of his young mother, carelessly throwing her life away without regard for her future son. He once wondered if Lena had been using while she was pregnant with him but had always been too afraid to ask.

"Jason," Sid said, standing. "Your mom wants to speak with you."

"Alone," Lena said. She wouldn't look away from Jason's face. Her thick eyebrows had contracted sharply over her hardened eyes, eyes that had become so unlike her once-nearly-a-twin sister's or the photos Jason saw of his grandfather.

"She wants to speak with you alone," Sid repeated. "Is that okay?"

"Yeah," Jason said. "It's okay."

Sid gave him that sad, close-lipped half-smile and left. Lena stared for a moment longer at Jason before throwing a manila envelope on the table.

"What the hell is this?" she asked.

Jason shrugged. "Why would I know?" he asked. Perhaps a bitter reaction, but could anyone blame him? Where the hell had she been? Jason caught a glimpse of her at Grandma Rebecca's funeral (which Aunt Claire paid for). Not once since then had she thought to check in on her son.

Lena slid a paper out of the envelope and said, "Your grandmother left you everything."

Jason moved closer to the table and picked up the paper. The car. The house. Enough money to pay tuition for Stanford and a flight to California. Jason fumbled with his words and semicoherently muttered, "I ... I didn't know ..."

"That bitch," Lena whispered.

Jason tensed. "Don't call her that."

"That's what she was," Lena said. "You don't know. She always thought she was a better mother than me. Always. She took my son."

"She didn't take me," Jason said. "I left."

"That's not true," Lena said. "It's not."

"It is."

"She wasn't always so perfect," Lena snapped. "You don't know. I have you, and all of a sudden she decides to be mother of the year." She laughed, high and cold and agonized, and Jason flinched. "She never stood up for me," Lena continued. "Never. After my dad died it was 'Silas this' and 'Silas that.' You probably wish he could have been there too. You have no idea what it was like. None." She put her head in her hands. Jason had never heard her talk about any of this before.

After a while, still looking down at the table and breathing hard, she said, "Do you remember when you and me went for ice cream that one time? You must have been four or five. You fell down on the sidewalk and scraped your knee. Not even hard, but you just cried and cried. I scooped you up and put you on a park bench and gave you water." She laughed to herself and said, "That's a trick. You tell the kid that if they don't drink water, they'll run out of tears, but they can't drink water and cry at the same time.

"You stopped crying, and I kissed your knee and said, 'All better?' And you nodded and smiled your little Jason smile and I got you vanilla chocolate swirl. It was your favorite. I had just gotten a job, and I was so damn proud I could pay for it without asking anyone for help." Her voice caught on the last word and she looked up at last, her eyes shining.

Jason couldn't remember ever seeing Lena cry before, not that she let him see. The rare times he caught her crying, he'd heard her through the wall or rounded the corner on her wiping her eyes right before she pretended nothing was wrong. He felt like he was intruding on something private, indecent.

Come to think of it, Jason didn't think he had cried in front of Lena in a long time, either. Perhaps not since the day of the ice cream.

"I tried to be good," she said. "I tried to be a good mother for you."

"I know you did," Jason lied. "I know."

Lena nodded and looked away. "I'm going to go." She gathered her tan coat from the back of the chair. The left sleeve had unraveled at the seam and a button had fallen off the cuff. She left without another word.

—

The day twelve-year-old Jason moved out of his childhood home, his mother was stoned to the point of incoherency.

Grandma Rebecca helped him with his things and reassured him that Lena, who hadn't made an appearance outside of her room in hours, would be okay without him. Where Rich was, Jason didn't know, nor did he care, but it would have been nice to know his mom wasn't alone when she was like this.

At home, his new home, Grandma Rebecca served him hot chocolate on the couch and tucked her knitted blue blanket around his shoulders.

"I don't know where I went so wrong with her," she said. "Claire is nothing like this."

Aunt Claire was a lawyer in DC. Her daughters were three and one and would probably never know what it was like to have a mother who dropped them off at school still drunk from the night before. Jason would meet them for the first time the following month, when Grandma Rebecca brought him to visit. He sipped his drink and nodded.

"I wish you could have known your mother when she was your age," Grandma Rebecca said. "She was so sweet. I really don't know ..." She trailed off and looked to Jason. "Are you doing all right?"

Jason nodded. "Thank you for letting me come live with you," he said quietly.

"Oh Jason," Grandma Rebecca said, "you'll always have a home here."

—

Sid drove Jason to the airport. He even walked Jason to security. "You'll come back for the holidays," he said. "Chawla and I will take care of it."

"Thank you," Jason said.

Sid pulled Jason into a hug and said, "I'm really proud of you." It didn't sound the same as when Grandma Rebecca had said it, but Jason said, "I know," because that was the right answer.

Sid clasped his shoulder. "I'll see you soon," he said. "I love you."

"I love you too," Jason said. It was the first time he had ever said that to Sid, he realized. What was more surprising, he meant it.

They had stayed up late talking the night before, sitting side by side on the couch in the living room without really looking at each other.

"We weren't in love," Sid told Jason, "but we were young and dumb and I was here for grad school. She left one day, and I moved on with my life like nothing had happened. I had never met your grandmother, but when she called me and told me who she was, she spoke to me like we were old friends. She wasn't angry. She believed me when I said I didn't know." Sid paused there, fiddling with the edge of his shirt sleeves. "I didn't," he continued, "but I suspected. When Lena moved all her stuff out and stopped talking to me. I've always hated myself for not asking. I think part of me didn't want to know."

Sid paused again, but Jason didn't say anything. He didn't know what to say. Maybe he should feel angry and perhaps he was a little, but if Jason had found himself in a similar situation, he didn't know what he would do.

When the silence had gone on for just a hair too long, Sid added, "It was one of the happiest days of my life, meeting you. My wedding, Ryan and Molly's births, and meeting you."

"I'm glad too," Jason said. They exchanged crooked smiles and Sid said, "Good."

On the flight, Jason re-read the letter his grandmother had written him, the one thing in the manilla envelope Lena hadn't touched. It was still sealed with a sticker, a faded blue butterfly with gold antennae. He ran his finger over the edge and read:

My dearest grandson,

Sweet Jason, if you're reading this, that means I'm dead, and you have my will. First, I want to say I hope you can forgive me. I always tried to do right by you, and I couldn't do that while paying for my heart meds. Please know that if there was another way, I would have taken it.

Of course, I'm sorry that I won't be able to be there for you and watch you grow and become the incredible man I know you will be, but I'm not sorry that I'm doing what I'm doing because I know that it will allow you to do so much more with your life and that you won't be alone. I've made a lot of choices I'm not sure of in my life. Many of them have to do with your mother. This is one of the few choices that I'm sure is right.

Regarding Lena: I want you to know that I do love her, truly, and I know she tries, but she didn't do right by you. I'm afraid that if you move back in with her, you'll never be allowed to leave. Maybe that's a terrible thing to say about my own daughter. But I can't let her be happy at your expense, especially since you moving back in won't make her happy. I don't know if anything will. My biggest hope for her is that she finds peace in herself, whatever that means. She loves you, too, even if she doesn't always know how to show it.

In Judaism, we don't say, "Rest in peace." We say, "May their memory be a blessing." I hope that's what I can be for you now. My Jason, you deserve a blessed life. I hope you can start to build your own in California.

I've left you everything. Sell what you need, and keep what you can. Whatever you do, live your life. I love you more than anything.
Grandma Rebecca

Chapter Three: Saturday
1971-1996

Zane was late. First, he overslept, which almost never happened. His internal clock (and often his children) woke him most days at six, sometimes five o'clock in the morning. Then, the car, which he'd intended to fill three days ago and every day since, needed gas. Last, he sat in heavy traffic, surrounded on all sides, for at least twenty minutes on his way to pick up the twins. Nearly an hour after he was supposed to show up, Zane pulled into the driveway in front of the one-story house at the end of the lane, white paint peeling despite his best attempts to keep the property intact.

Noah was on him before he could shut the car door, skinny six-year-old limbs sticking out of a faded Balto T-shirt. "Daddy! Daddy, where were you?"

"Sitting in traffic," he said, setting Noah on his hip. "Where's your sister?" Recently, Zane's kids had grown nearly too heavy to carry.

Noah shrugged, already wriggling to get down. Zane set him on the ground and Noah shot off to the house. Not the home Zane had grown up in. That house was situated on the edge of Brooklyn Heights and had sold three years ago to a young, pregnant, obscenely in love couple Zane couldn't look at for too long without hyperventilating. The wife, thin and Black with straightened hair, looked nothing like his Helena, with her wild curls and scattered freckles across swaths of pale skin, but Zane couldn't help but see his wife in this woman he hardly knew.

Inside, Zane greeted Miranda, who was coloring at the kitchen table, with a kiss on the head. "How was your visit?"

"Good," she said. "Grandpa Fred let us watch a movie."

"Fun." Zane's father came into the kitchen. "Thank you for watching them," Zane said.

His father waved a hand in dismissal. "I love having them here," his father told him in lightly accented but fluent English. Truly, he would probably watch the twins more often if Zane allowed it, if the guilt didn't threaten to consume him every time he left them behind.

"Have you heard from Lena recently?"

Zane frowned at the sudden change of topic. "No?"

"Rebecca can't get ahold of her." Lena was technically his cousin's daughter, his second cousin or his cousin once removed or something along those lines, but he was closer in age to Lena than her mother. Lena's son wasn't much older than the twins and would come by, on occasion, when Lena sent him to stay with her mother while she was off getting high somewhere. It was supposed to be a family secret, but within the family, everyone knew. Zane hadn't spoken to Lena in over a year.

Zane opened his mouth to say so when Miranda cut him off. "Daddy," she said, "I'm hungry."

"Do you want to stay for lunch?" Zane's father asked. It was a tempting offer. Zane hadn't been able to shop this week and their food supply consisted of store-brand chocolate milk,

Froot Loops, and Eggo waffles. On the other hand, guilt sat like a stone in his stomach. *He* was Noah and Miranda's dad, for crying out loud. He could stop at a store and buy a box of Annie's mac and cheese instead of passing the responsibility off on his own father.

Zane was about to protest that they were all right when Noah rocketed into the room. "Can we Daddy? Please?"

It *would* take a burden off his shoulders. Plus, he hadn't spent time with his father outside of temple in too long. "All right, all right." Zane set a hand on Noah's head.

To his father he said, "If you really don't mind."

His father waved a hand. "You can help," he said.

.

After two hours and many pleas from the children to stay, Zane had both kids at home and *The Little Mermaid* on the speakers while Noah and Miranda played in the living room. It was a soundtrack he grudgingly had to admit was better than some of the others he'd been subjected to over the years. A call came as Ariel launched into the last chorus of "Part of Your World," prompting Zane to pause it and Noah to go, "Aww."

Zane grinned to himself and picked up the phone. "Hello?"

"Hey, are you busy tonight?"

Abby Chen, Zane's best friend from undergrad. She never introduced herself on a call. Never a, "Hey, it's Abby," but Zane always knew who it was. She was the only one he knew who barreled into a conversation the way she always did. He glanced back at his kids. "I just picked up Noah and Miranda. Is everything ok?"

"D'you remember my brother?" she asked. "He's moved back to Westchester and he was asking about you, so I thought I'd ask if you wanted to join us for dinner."

Vaguely, Zane recalled a cheerful, dark-eyed man always chatting with strangers wherever they happened to go and coming away with at least one new friend. He was two years older than Abby, so a year older than Zane, and studying at NYU at the time, but he visited California on breaks. Zane always liked him, enjoyed his visits, but he couldn't say they were ever friends. "That's ... sweet of him. Next weekend, maybe? Is this a standing invite?"

"Next weekend sounds fantastic," Abby said. "I'll tell Henry."

"Daddy," Noah piped up, "I want to see Abby." Miranda eyed the phone warily and didn't say anything. She usually didn't speak whenever anyone else was around besides her brother, father, and grandfather. She wouldn't even speak to Abby, whom they'd known their whole lives, whom Zane considered family. When they were together, Noah would sometimes speak for Miranda like they were one person.

"Maybe next time," Zane said to Noah.

To Abby, he said, "I'll see you next week."

.

Most of Zane's current friends were from college. Abby and their whole group, though he and Abby were the only ones in New York. Most of their clique, for lack of a better word, had settled in or around San Francisco, but Zane and Abby had both grown up in New York and both found jobs in-state. In undergrad, they would fly home together for the holidays, or else cross-country road trip as they did one memorable winter break Zane's junior and Abby's sophomore year. They'd slept in the car at night and ate mostly pre-packaged sandwiches and chips from their dorm's vending machine. By the time they got home, both of their stomachs ached with hunger and his father lectured him for at least an hour about healthy eating habits.

Zane met his wife in undergrad. He had signed up to tutor French his first semester, though he'd tested out of having to take the class. His first student was one Helena Rubin, who teased him from the first. "Aren't you a freshman?" she asked, twisting long, wild hair between her fingers.

"I'm good at languages," he said. His parents, both German, spoke it around the house, and Zane had become nearly fluent in French while studying abroad for a semester in high school.

"Excellent," Helena said. "I have no clue what I'm doing."

Unfortunately for Helena's French grade, they spent far more time flirting in their sessions than they did studying. She introduced him to the Jewish group on campus and teased him gently for adhering so strictly to his kosher diet now that he was on his own. She had a car on campus and took them downtown more and more frequently as the semester progressed, to restaurants and parks. Just to get away from the dorms, she said. It took Zane an embarrassingly long time to realize those trips were dates.

Helena assumed Zane didn't have his license because he was from Brooklyn, and for a while, he let her believe that was the reason. She stopped teasing him about it after she learned he had deeper reasons for refusing to get behind the wheel. He hated that it still affected him so much, so many years after his mother's accident. His father tried to get Zane to take a permit test his senior year of high school, until Zane sat in the driver's seat for his first lesson and immediately began hyperventilating. It took four years before they tried again.

Helena's parents had fled Hungary after World War II, just like Zane's parents had fled Germany at the start. Helena's parents didn't speak any Hungarian at home, though. "So I'm hopelessly monolingual," she told him. By the end of the semester, Helena got a B- in French, and Zane got a girlfriend.

Zane couldn't think about those first weeks together without thinking about blood splattered on carpet, about open, glazed eyes staring up at the ceiling, unseeing. About the screams, searing and forever intertwined with previously comforting memories of his wife.

The first few weeks after losing her, Zane might as well have been in a trance. One moment he was accepting condolences at her Shiva, the next getting the then three-year-old twins ready for a bath with no time in between. His father tried to help, to get Zane to talk to him or anyone really. It hurt him, to see Zane in such a state, and to Zane, that made everything worse. His father, who'd lost Zane's mother when Zane was only ten, was the only one who'd understood what it was like, had moved out to Westchester to be closer to Zane and the kids after Helena died, but not even that harrowing connection could pull Zane out of his depression.

Abby came over every few days and made sure he ate with the kids. "She'd hate to see you like this," Abby said. Her eyes were raw and red and Zane couldn't look at them. He hadn't been able to spend time with their old college friends at the funeral, and not because he didn't have the time.

"She'll never have to," Zane said, blinking back tears. He'd cried more these last few weeks than the rest of his life put together, including when his mother died. The tears just kept coming.

"You have to eat," Abby said. Zane shrugged, and Abby crossed her arms. "Zane."

"I keep seeing her," he whispered. Her hair fanned out behind her head and blood seeping into the pale brown carpet. The image made him dizzy, and he closed his eyes, sucking in a shallow, shaky breath.

"The kids are scared," Abby said. "Or, Noah is. I can't get two words out of Miranda, but he swears she is too."

Zane frowned. "They are?"

"Obviously," Abby scoffed. "So am I. You look like a zombie."

He looked away again. "I don't know what to do."

Abby didn't say anything. What could she say that would make it better? Instead, she pulled his head onto her shoulder and put an arm around him. They stayed like that for a long while, until Noah called for him in the other room and Zane forced himself off the couch.

—

The week before dinner at Abby's went by at odd intervals. The days crawled and the evenings flew, and Zane found himself looking forward to the evening with his friend and this Henry Chen he'd simultaneously heard so much and so little about in the interim. Henry studied biology at NYU, Abby told him, but she also mentioned he wasn't working right now. No kids. No partner.

Zane's father took Miranda and Noah after temple on Saturday morning. Every week, he brought the kids back to his house, to spend time with his grandkids and give Zane a true day of rest. The first time he'd done it, Zane hadn't known what to do with himself, the house so terrifyingly quiet in the absence of toddler screeches and no Helena absentmindedly humming to herself. Zane got blackout drunk on old Scotch and rum until morning and told his father he just had a terrible headache when he went to pick up the kids on Sunday. His father had put a hand on his shoulder and said, "You do what you need to get through it."

It had gotten easier since then. Sometimes, he could even go whole weekends without thinking about Helena. Much.

Saturday evening, Zane showed up to Abby's with a bottle of white wine and rang the doorbell. Henry answered with a wide grin. He looked just like Zane remembered: dark, shining eyes and a bright smile just like Abby's. "Zane! Come in. It's great to see you. I'm almost done cooking."

"What a relief," Zane said. "I'd resigned myself to Abby's cooking and a night of food poisoning." Henry laughed, and Zane grinned.

"What is it you're up to these days?" Henry asked, leading him to the kitchen.

"I run the Hebrew school," Zane told him. "Judea Reform."

"That must be a handful with twins."

So Abby had been talking, or else Henry had asked before they met up.

"A bit," Zane admitted. It meant he could be home roughly when Miranda and Noah got off school, but it didn't pay well, and he constantly took on freelance editing projects he could do from home. His father, too, had put off retirement to help with the kids financially, to contribute whenever they grew out of another pair of shoes or needed to supply a box of colored pencils for their classroom at school. Another weight Zane carried.

"Were you an education major at SF?"

"International studies and English, actually. Life is weird like that." And then, to be polite, he asked, "What have you been up to? You were studying biology at NYU, weren't you?" Thank you to Abby for filling him in.

Speaking of Abby. "He went on to get a PhD in autoimmune diseases," she said, entering the kitchen. "Hey, you."

"Hi, Abs." He turned back to Henry. "That's very impressive," Zane said, taking a seat. "Why autoimmune diseases?"

"Our dad had MS," Abby said. "Multiple sclerosis."

Henry poured himself a glass of wine. "I was diagnosed a few months ago," he said quietly.

Zane barely kept his jaw shut. Wasn't MS deadly? How could this vibrant, engaging man Zane's own age be so well acquainted with his own mortality? He scanned Henry briefly for signs of the disease, though he didn't know exactly what he was looking for, then stopped himself before Henry caught him.

"That must have been hard for you," Zane said. No "I'm so sorry" or "That's awful!" People said that to him plenty after Helena died. He had never wanted their pity. Henry probably wouldn't either. He had to stop himself from giving it anyway.

Henry shrugged. "I struggled for a while. I'm doing better now." That would explain why Henry came back to New York. He met Zane's eyes with his own, deep and bright, and Zane had the distinct feeling he was being X-rayed. "Sorry," Henry said. "I didn't mean to unload on you."

"You didn't," Zane said. "I'm interested." For a beat, it was impossible to look away.

Abby cleared her throat and the spell was broken. Both men turned to her. "What?" Henry asked.

"Nothing," Abby said. "I'm still here. Thought I'd let you know."

"Oh come on, Abby."

"My apologies," Zane said. "Do *you* have any incurable chronic illnesses Abby?" Abby muttered something incoherent, and Henry failed to suppress another smile.

.

They talked for hours about anything and everything. Politics. Music. Embarrassing stories about Abby, who took it all in stride. Henry was smart, and witty, and Zane didn't think he'd laughed so hard in years. Every once in a while, Abby made an offhand comment about how they were cute together, which they both ignored, or pretended to ignore. It was nearly midnight by the time Henry got up to use the bathroom and Abby leaned over the table. "Holy shit."

Zane frowned. "What?"

"You," she said. "And Henry."

Zane feigned ignorance. "What about me and Henry?"

"He's not bad on the eyes, don't you think?"

"God, Abby, he's your brother."

"I'm just saying, you could cut the sexual tension in here with a knife. He likes men too, you know." Henry returned then and Abby sat back in her seat, resuming a painfully innocent expression that hadn't fooled Zane since undergrad.

Her words resonated in his head the whole drive home. *You, and Henry.* Ridiculous. Zane was, in fact, bi, but that wasn't the point. He had already had the great love of his life. No one could replace Helena.

In spite of this, Zane couldn't banish Henry's eyes from his mind.

.

Three days after dinner at Abby's, Zane arrived home late and had just paid the babysitter, a high-school junior who lived three houses down and whom Zane had coached through her Bat Mitzvah three or four years prior, when the phone rang.

"IgotitIgotit," Noah yelled, barreling down the hallway. He picked up the phone and pressed it hard against his face. "Hello?" A beat, and he held it out to Zane. "Daddy, it's for you."

"Can you ask who it is?"

"He said Henry," Noah told him. Zane's stomach did a cart-wheel.

He took the phone, and Noah ran off again. "Hi."

"Hey, Abby gave me your number. I hope you don't mind."

"Not at all," Zane said. He sat on the edge of the armchair, stretching the phone cord as far as it would go.

"I wanted to call and say I had a great time the other night. It hasn't been easy for me recently, and you were kind of a bright spot in all of this." Henry went quiet on the other end, but before Zane could say anything, Henry added, "That sounds strange. Sorry. I just … thank you."

"Of course," Zane said. He bit his lip, drafting and redrafting what he wanted to say in his mind. He should invite Henry over, right? It was only polite. But what would Henry think of his toy-strewn house? What if he really was just calling to say thank you?

"Well, that was really all, so I'll let you go …"

"I had a great time too," Zane blurted before Henry hung up. "I'd love to make you dinner in return, if you're around this weekend."

"I would love that," Henry said immediately. "Let me know when and where and I'll be there."

They settled on a time and Zane gave him the address. They hung up and Zane gripped the back of the chair, just breathing. He was being ridiculous, of course. This was just a friend thing. Two friends, hanging out and … Though making dinner was rather romantic, wasn't it?

.

That Saturday after temple, Zane perseverated for hours over what to wear. He debated calling Abby for advice but nixed that idea almost immediately. This was her brother, for crying out loud. Besides, he was an adult. He could dress for a night in with a friend. He was being ridiculous.

He settled on a sky-blue sweater three minutes before Henry was due to show up, tucking away the pale green button up that had been Helena's favorite. When Henry knocked (fifteen minutes later, so there truly hadn't been a need to rush), Zane pulled the door open and Henry eyed him up and down.

"You look nice," he said. Zane nearly melted on the spot.

Saturdays became the highlight of his week. Every weekend, Henry would go to Zane's place or Zane would come to Henry's. On those nights, Abby was always conspicuously absent. One weekend they both decided they didn't feel like cooking and Zane introduced Henry to the Hungarian place he used to go to with Helena, accompanied by a small pang of guilt he couldn't entirely ignore.

He opened up to Henry perhaps more than he'd opened up to anyone before Helena or since. He shared about his mother's death, the stories she used to tell before bedtime, and the twist in his gut when he used to wake up before school and she wouldn't be there. He talked about his relationship with his father, a man who had to be both parents to a bitter and emotionally bruised pre-teen and never once complained.

"It's wonderful you two were close," Henry said.

"We still are. He watches the kids every week, after services."

"Are you all religious? I know you run the Hebrew school."

"Not really. More … It's a community, I suppose. My father escaped Germany during the Second World War, so it means more to him. But I don't know that he believes in a god."

Henry, too, told Zane about how his mother had remarried just a year after his father died, when Henry was sixteen, and how his stepfather had been especially hard on Abby. Their mother was older, and when she died, it was almost a relief. He told Zane about his own diagnosis. "There are treatments," he said hesitantly. "More than there were for my father."

"It's ok to be scared," Zane said.

Henry gave a shaky laugh. "Sometimes it doesn't feel that way," he said. "People are always telling me to be brave or admire me for being so strong." He put the last two words in air quotes.

"People said the same to me after my wife died," Zane said.

"How did she die?" It should have been an invasive question, perhaps, but coming from Henry, it was different. It was genuine, and Zane wanted him to know. He told Henry about visiting Helena's family in Pittsburgh. A long time coming, Helena's mother said at the time. They'd left the kids with his father so he and Helena could take a rare weekend to themselves, but promised Helena's parents they would bring them next time.

He spoke about going with them to temple in the morning, about the gunman and the subsequent shooting. He didn't share the image he carried in his head of Helena on the ground, still, already brain-dead, though he wouldn't know it for hours. He didn't tell Henry about the aftermath, about Helena dying a second time in the hospital or Zane coming home to his kids, having to tell them their mother was gone, or about the bottomless depression and the familiar rage. Not yet, at least.

Still, the former had been enough to turn Henry pale white. "Christ. That's ... I don't know what to say to that."

Zane nodded. "Me neither," he said.

.

One week, perhaps a month after Zane re-met Henry at Abby's place, Zane's Aunt Gabi planned to visit for the weekend.

Which was great, really, but it did mean he had to make a call. When he got Henry on the phone, he said, "My aunt is visiting this weekend, so I'll have the kids Saturday night. Rain check?"

"Of course," Henry said. "Or, I wouldn't mind dinner with them, but I can also wait until next week if it's too much."

Zane bit his lip to keep himself from smiling at the thought of Henry meeting his kids. Miranda would be a tough sell, of course, but she would come around eventually, and Noah would love him immediately. "If you don't mind spaghetti or mac and cheese," he said, "we'd love to have you this weekend."

Zane spent the rest of the week in a state of semi-euphoria, even through three freelance deadlines and Noah's sudden low-grade fever. He smiled so much at work the rabbi asked who had him grinning like that. He imagined over and over what the meeting would be like, until he woke up Saturday morning feeling like an anvil had struck his skull. He sat up against the pillows, his head reeling and his stomach churning. The clock told him it was just past nine, far later than Zane had slept in years. The kids would be up by now, probably watching cartoons until Zane got up to make them breakfast. He threw the blankets back and shivered violently. Just his luck. He didn't have *time* to be ill.

First, he poured Froot Loops in one bowl for Miranda, Cheerios in another for Noah (who was sick of Froot Loops), trying his best not to breathe on the food. Then, he called his father to say he was ill and wouldn't be seeing them at temple or joining them in the afternoon. Last, he called Henry.

"Do you need anything?" Henry asked when Zane explained that he couldn't host this evening.

"I'm all right," he said. He winced. His throat burned.

"You sound terrible," he said. "Can I bring you soup, at least?"

"I don't want to bother you," Zane rasped.

"It wouldn't be a bother," Henry said. "I'll be over soon."

In the intervening hour or so, Zane fell asleep on the couch and woke to Henry's gentle hand on his shoulder. "Hey."

Zane stirred and winced. "Henry?" He opened his eyes a crack and put a hand to his throbbing head. Somewhere in the distance, he heard Abby and Noah's voices, but they were fuzzy, like they might come through on a badly tuned radio.

"How're you feeling?" Henry said softly.

Zane groaned and pressed his hands to his eyes. "Head hurts," he rasped. Bright red stars bloomed across his vision.

Henry put a cool hand over Zane's forehead. "You're burning up," he said. "Let's get you to bed, all right?"

"The kids ..."

"Abby will watch them," Henry said. "Actually ..." He turned to the kitchen and called, "Hey, Abs?"

Abby poked her head in. "Damn, Zane, you look like death."

"Thank you, Abby," Henry said pointedly. "Watch the twins. I'm taking him to bed." Henry helped Zane into a sitting position, and Zane leaned heavily against Henry in return. Henry slipped an arm around him and half-helped, half-dragged Zane down the hallway. A pair of wide hazel eyes peered out at them from behind one of the doors and Henry tried to smile at Miranda, but she slammed the door once she realized he'd seen her.

Hot nausea clawed its way from Zane's stomach to his throat and he broke away, scrambling for the bathroom. He retched over the toilet and shivered at the sudden lack of Henry's body heat. Henry followed him and sat at the edge of the tub and rubbed Zane's back in slow circles. "How did you get so sick?"

Zane shuddered and spat the taste of bile out of his mouth. "Noah had a fever earlier this week," he said. "But it wasn't like this."

"I don't think Noah's been running himself ragged quite like you've been," Henry said. He wasn't wrong. Between work and his freelance projects and Noah being sick and helping Miranda with school and checking in on his father and doing the house-work, Zane hadn't slept more than four hours a night in days.

Henry stayed with him until he was done heaving and helped Zane to the bedroom after. Zane collapsed on top of the blan-kets, still shaking. Henry crouched beside the bed. "Do you need anything? Water?"

"Can't," Zane said. He shut his eyes against the harsh light from the uncovered window. "Can't keep it down."

"Well you're going to have to try or you're going to get dehy-drated," Henry said. "Please? For me?"

Zane's eyes drifted closed. "All right," he said.

.

Helena was beautiful in her wedding dress. She floated in and out of Zane's fevered dreams, elusive and trailing a familiar lace train. As soon as he got close to her, she'd vanish again, only to reappear around a corner, just out of reach. He chased her, fingers catching on the tail end of the train, until at last he managed to catch hold of her arm, and then she was falling into his, only Helena wasn't Helena anymore but Henry, and his blood was darkening the pale brown carpet...

A slamming door broke through Zane's dream, and his eyes snapped open. His T-shirt had soaked through with sweat and his blankets twisted tightly around his legs. Vaguely, he recalled Henry in his room all day and night before, making sure he drank and helping him to the bathroom.

Decidedly *not* bleeding out on the floor of a Pittsburgh sanctuary. Zane licked his cracked lips and swallowed around the painful ball in his throat.

His bedroom door opened halfway and Henry peered in. "You're awake."

"Yeah." Zane rubbed his eyes. His brain felt somehow too light and too heavy all at once. The dream fading quickly, but the horror of seeing Henry dying in his arms wouldn't leave him.

Henry felt his forehead, sending chills up Zane's arm for more than one reason. "You're still warm," he said. "How are you feeling?"

"Better than yesterday," Zane said. His voice was still hoarse, a whisper, but it didn't ache to speak like it had the day before. "Thank you for being here."

"It's no trouble," Henry said immediately. "I made the kids a very nutritious breakfast of sugar cereal and chocolate milk. They were worried about you, especially Miranda, but I think I convinced them you were all right."

"Wait ... Miranda spoke to you?" He couldn't remember the last time Miranda spoke to a new person. Just a few weeks prior their new cantor had said hello to them after Hebrew school and Miranda hid in Zane's office for ten minutes.

"It took a while," Henry said. "I just gave her some space, and she opened up eventually."

"That's amazing," Zane said. He sat up a little straighter and inhaled sharply. He still had a headache just behind his eyes, but it was duller. Someone (probably Henry) had refilled the glass of water on the bedside table. Zane took a long drink. "Did you stay here all night?" he asked. There was nowhere else to sleep but the couch. Or maybe Henry hadn't slept, judging by the dark circles under his eyes.

"It's all right," Henry said. "You would have done the same."

"Thank you," Zane said again. "I feel like we haven't been friends long enough for you to watch me throw up."

Henry waved a hand. "I took care of my dad toward the end. Sickness doesn't bother me." It was supposed to be reassuring, but all Zane could think was that Henry had the same disease, the illness that killed his father, that he could very well fall ill at any time. In the wake of his dream, the thought was even more horrifying.

Zane shoved it aside. "You should rest though," he said, "or you'll be coming down with this next."

"Will you call me later? Let me know how you're doing?"

"I will," Zane said. "Thank you."

"You don't have to thank me," Henry said with a wink. "I'll see you soon, Zane."

—

Nearly a decade ago, Helena sat behind Zane on the bed and wrapped her arms around his shoulders. "I need to talk to you," she said.

He turned to face her and found her normally bright expression solemn. "What is it?" he asked. Her parents were fine as far as he knew, as was her sister. His father was doing well. It was two weeks until their wedding. What could possibly make her beautiful face so grave?

"I want to talk about what happens if something, you know, happens," she said. "To either of us."

A cold weight dropped in the pit of Zane's stomach. "Why do we need to have this conversation now?" he asked. They were twenty-six. They were both healthy. Zane's mom had died young, but she'd been in a car accident. Nothing genetic.

"Because we're getting married," Helena said. "Because I want to make sure we'd both be ok if one of us died."

Zane squirmed. "I don't know what I'd do without you," he said. They had been together for nearly eight years. It felt like his whole life.

"Please, can we talk about this? For me?"

"You can't just say 'for me' and expect me to do what you want," he said. She pouted, and Zane resisted the urge to laugh. Barely. "All right, all right."

"If I died," she said, ignoring Zane's wince, "I'd want you to move on." He opened his mouth to speak and Helena said, "I'm not finished. Give it a reasonable mourning period, obviously. Don't let people think you were having an affair." Zane rolled his eyes, and Helena said, "It's important, Zane."

"I don't want to think about life without you," Zane said quietly.

"You won't have to," Helena said. "Hopefully not for a very, very long time."

Years later, nearly two years after the life-altering and devastating events in Pittsburgh, Miranda asked him, "Are you going to get married again ever?"

Zane could only gape at her. She'd been watching TV when the question came out of seemingly nowhere. "I ... I don't know. I don't have any plans to get married," he said. Miranda, who was five at the time, nodded and Zane continued, "Why do you ask?"

"Jamie's parents are divorced and her dad is getting married this weekend."

Helena's face swam to the forefront of his mind. She was laughing, her head flung back and her eyes crinkled with delight. Zane fought the urge to throw up or scream or burst into tears and said, "I'm not divorced."

79

He wondered how much Miranda even remembered of her mother. There were dozens of photos all around the house and he told the kids about her all the time, but they'd been so young when Helena died. He wondered if Miranda even recognized the difference between divorced and widowed.

"I was just wondering," Miranda said. "Can we have dessert?" The transition gave him utter whiplash, but he tried not to show it. "Viviana told me she gave you dessert before she left," Zane said of their then-babysitter. Miranda pouted and Zane said, "Tomorrow night, schatz. I'll make you your favorite." Bienenstich, the sweet bee sting cake his father used to make. When he'd have time to do that, he didn't know, but Miranda smiled a smile so reminiscent of her mother and Zane knew he would do whatever it took to make her happy.

—

The Saturday following his illness, Zane cooked lasagne for Henry as a thank you. "Miranda hasn't stopped talking about you all week," Zane said.

Henry flashed him another one of his disarming smiles. They were on the couch post-meal, red wine in shallow glasses. "Anytime, really. Even if you just need someone to watch them. They're sweet kids."

"I appreciate that," Zane said. There was a not-entirely-uncomfortable flush creeping up his cheeks. He told himself it was from the wine, or perhaps a lingering fever.

Henry set his drink on the table. "Can I ask you something?" Zane nodded, and Henry said, "I don't want to read into things and you can tell me to forget it, but … What exactly is this?" He gestured between them.

The room went cold. "What is what?" Zane's chest tightened and his breaths grew shallow.

"What are we doing, Zane? I don't want to read into things," Henry said again, "but it seems like maybe this is more than a friendship." It shouldn't have been a question, but the upward inflection at the end of the sentence suggested otherwise.

"I ... I don't—I've thought about it," he admitted.

"And?"

And you're dying. "I do like you," Zane said quietly. "A lot." He couldn't think. He couldn't breathe.

Henry arched an eyebrow. "But?"

Zane shrugged, and Henry put a hand on his knee. "If you're not ready for this, I'll leave right now. But if you are, know that I'd really like to kiss you."

Zane couldn't help but laugh. "You're perfect, you know?" *And dying. He's dying.*

"I've heard that," Henry teased. "I like you too, Zane." Slowly, Zane nodded, and Henry slid his hand up to Zane's thigh, and then Zane leaned forward and they were kissing, and kissing, and for the first time in three years, Zane didn't feel so alone.

—

He wasn't late getting his kids that Sunday, but he ended up staying at his father's a while anyway. Zane sat in the kitchen with a mug of tea in his hands while Miranda and Noah played outside in the newly fallen snow. "Did Rebecca ever get ahold of Lena, by the way?" She constantly disappeared, but Lena always came back. So far, at least.

His father gave him a searching look, but said, "Yes. She's agreed to go to rehab."

"Good," Zane said. He ran a finger over the skin where his wedding ring used to sit. It had taken him a year to remove it, and only at the insistence of his father, who promised he'd done the same when Zane's mother died. Zane kept the ring in a drawer beside his bed now, in a velvet-lined box, but the skin it used to occupy had never quite lost its pale discoloration.

"Are you all right?" his father asked. "You're … far away."

Zane shrugged. "I have a lot on my mind," he said, but he didn't. Zane had one very specific person on his mind, and he couldn't seem to cast him out. The previous night had been wonderful, and terrifying, and he'd woken up thinking of Helena. He took a breath. "Rebecca must be happy."

"Is it Abby?"

Zane nearly choked on his tea. "I—what? My friend Abby?"

"You've always been close," his father said with a shrug.

"No," Zane said. "Abby isn't interested in anyone like that."

"Really?"

"Yes," Zane said, a bit defensively. Abby had always been outwardly confident, but she'd worried for years that her lack of sexual attraction to anyone meant something was wrong with her. Zane was one of the few she confided in.

Probably Henry was too.

Zane liked Henry. More than he should for the little time they'd known each other. He liked laughing at Henry's corny jokes and the butterflies in his chest when Henry called and the way Henry smiled at him when Zane pulled out a chair or offered him more wine, like Zane was the center of his world. And yet, how could he put his kids through that? Could he watch a partner die twice and maintain some semblance of his already fragmented sanity?

"You know, if there was someone in your life," his father said, "that would be ok." Zane sipped his drink slowly and his father continued, "I know it feels wrong. I felt that way after your mother died." As far as Zane knew, his father hadn't started dating again until Zane was in college.

"Why are we having this conversation now, Dad?"

"You've been very happy these last few weeks," his father said with a crooked smile. A smile Zane had inherited, that he saw in his aunt on the rare occasions she did smile. "And then you show up today looking like someone killed your cat."

"I don't have a cat."

"You know what I'm saying."

"It's a little more complicated than that," Zane said.

"Of course it's complicated, but there is too much tragedy in this world not to be happy when you have the chance."

Zane took a breath. "What if he's dying?"

His father's face fell. "Oh, Zane."

The empathy in his father's voice nearly sent him over the edge. "He has MS," Zane said, his voice taught with suppressed tears. "I don't know if I can go through that again."

His father exhaled through his nose, slowly. "He's definitely dying?"

It struck Zane, for the millionth time in these last few weeks, how little he knew about the disease. "His father died from it," Zane said. "He told me there are treatments, but I don't know..."

"I can't tell you what to do," his father said, "but I only got fourteen years with my parents and I wouldn't trade them for the world. My brother, he was eleven when I left Germany and I've never regretted loving him. And if I knew from the beginning that my time with your mother was limited, I would have wanted to be with her anyway for what little time we had." He patted Zane's knee once, twice, then rested a hand on Zane's leg. "Don't wait too long," he warned, just as Noah and Miranda came barreling inside, demanding hot cocoa with cinnamon.

.

For the rest of the week, Zane ignored Henry's calls. He ignored Abby's calls. He forgot to finish tasks at work, spaced out in the middle of conversations with his colleagues and once with a prospective parent looking to enroll her kids in the Hebrew school. Three different people asked him if he was ok. No, he wasn't, but what was he supposed to tell them?

If he were Henry, he'd be furious right now. Zane was stringing him along, punishing him for something out of his control. He tried to convince himself he didn't even like Henry that much anyway. Or maybe Henry was stringing *him* along. Maybe he made everyone feel that warm ball in their chest, made everyone want to open themselves up to him and bleed their secrets at his feet. Unlikely, but possible. He had to hold on to something or risk falling apart completely.

At last, on Saturday again, Zane summoned the courage to go over to Henry's place. He would turn Henry down. He would say he was sorry, but he wasn't ready for a relationship, and he wished Henry well.

Then he was standing on Henry's doorstep and Henry wrenched the door open, staring with wide and too forgiving eyes. The words died in Zane's throat. "Hi," he managed.

"Are you ok?" Henry asked. "You haven't been answering my calls, or Abby's."

Zane looked at Henry's feet. "I've been blowing you off all week, and the first thing you ask me is if I'm all right?"

Henry laughed nervously. "Well."

"You should be angry with me."

"Maybe," Henry said. "I've never been quick to anger."

"I stood you up."

"We didn't have plans."

Zane pressed a hand to his forehead to stave off an oncoming headache. It didn't work.

Henry frowned. "Would you like me to be angry with you?"

"No." Though it might be easier, he had to admit.

"I really like you, Zane. But if this can't go anywhere, I need to know that."

"I'm sorry." He took a breath. "I really like you too. I just ..." Zane took a breath. "I don't know if I can watch someone I care about die again."

The air between them grew thick, tense, and not the kind of tense Abby liked to tease them about. "Oh." Henry took a step back. His face went from open concern to impassive in the blink of an eye.

"I don't mean ... I don't know what I mean."

"MS isn't a death sentence. I'll be sick, but it doesn't have to mean I'll die."

"I can't—" The possibility, just the idea that it could happen again, left Zane breathless and dizzy. "I'm sorry."

"I don't know what to do then," Henry said. His words carried a sharp edge Zane had never heard before. "I'll never not be sick."

"I know that."

"If you're not ready for that, then you're not."

"I want to be," Zane said. "I'm so sorry."

"I knew this would happen," Henry said softly. "When I was diagnosed. But I'd hoped you would ..." he trailed off and gripped his arms in a poor imitation of a hug.

"I want to be with you," Zane said again. "I just can't."

A pause. Henry turned his eyes back to Zane. "That's it, then."

Zane swallowed hard. "I don't want that either."

"Well you can't have both," Henry snapped. "Believe me, if I could have avoided an MS diagnosis I would have."

I've never been quick to anger, he'd said, but Zane had crossed a line. "I'm so sorry."

"I don't want your pity," Henry said, his voice strained. "I never did. I just wanted to spend time with you. Take things slow."

Wanted, not want. "All right. I'll go, then."

Henry didn't say anything, and Zane turned to leave. He looked back halfway down the drive. Henry hadn't shut the door yet, was just staring after him, and Zane felt, in the pit of his stomach, that he was making a huge mistake. Then Henry did shut the door and it didn't matter anymore.

.

Zane hadn't gotten so drunk since the first night he'd spent alone after Helena died, when his father took the kids. The first bit of vodka reassured him, warmed his stomach, made him feel like he may have done the right thing. A little while after that, the alcohol turned on him, forced him to think of the man he'd turned away and all he'd given up. Henry's warm smile. His deep laugh. The way he made Zane feel like he was flying. Then Zane was too incoherent to think many thoughts at all.

His father tried to talk to him about it the next morning, but Zane shrugged him off. He took the kids and spent the rest of the day chugging water and popping Advil. Between taking care of his kids and feeling like utter garbage, Zane couldn't spare a thought (or very many at least) for Henry. Monday, though, every doubt came flooding back, and with them the anguish. It had only been a day and he missed Henry so badly it made his chest ache. Monday turned to Tuesday, and by Wednesday, even his kids noticed something was off. At dinner that night Miranda asked, "Are you getting sick again Daddy?"

Zane shook his head. "Just tired, hon. I'm all right." Miranda frowned and Zane immediately thought she wore a too-serious expression for such a young face.

·

He missed Henry so badly it hurt. At night, Zane pressed his hands against his aching heart, willing his thoughts to turn from the never-ending loop of Henry pressing rough kisses to his neck and Henry running a cool palm over his fevered forehead and the shocked agony on Henry's face when Zane turned him away. Briefly, Zane considered sleeping pills, but what if his kids needed him in the night?

He had to talk to Henry.

Saturday morning at temple, after the Kaddish, Zane's father put a hand on his jittering leg. Zane hadn't even realized he'd been shaking it. He put a reassuring hand over his father's (when had his father's skin become so thin?) and resumed his unseeing stare toward the front of the sanctuary.

After the service, he left his kids in the company of his father with a kiss for each of them. He left for Henry's, nearly turning around at least twice. He hesitated at the door, wondering if it wouldn't be better for both of them if Zane disappeared from Henry's life before Zane hurt him again, but Zane had never been that selfless. He knocked twice and waited, heart in his throat.

It wasn't Henry who opened the door this time, but Abby. Her eyebrow furrowed and she crossed her arms. "What do you want?"

"Is Henry here?"

"He doesn't want to talk to you."

"It's ok, Abby." Henry came up behind her and peered at Zane through a pair of thick, rectangular glasses Zane had never seen before. Abby looked back and forth between the two of them, then threw up her hands in defeat before stalking off. Henry leaned against the doorway. "What do you want?" he asked. Uncanny how he sounded so like Abby in the moment.

Zane picked at his nail. "Those are new." He nodded at the glasses. "They suit you."

"Yeah, it's an MS thing," Henry said sharply.

Zane tried not to wince. He cleared his throat. "I messed up."

Henry crossed his arms over his chest. "You were an ass."

"I was. I don't have the right to ask you this, but if you would be open to it ... I'd like to see you again."

Henry exhaled slowly. "You're ready to watch me die, then?"

"I never should have said that."

"No, you shouldn't have," Henry said. "What's changed?"

Zane shook his head. "Nothing. I missed you. I want to be with you."

Henry fixed him with a long, hard stare. "I will never not be sick. You know that, right?"

"I know," Zane said. "But ... It wasn't that. I don't—I'm scared, Henry, but I want this. I want you."

"You using my diagnosis to reject me just because you were scared doesn't make me feel better. You know that, right?" Zane nodded, and Henry uncrossed his arms. He fiddled with his sweater sleeve. "I should say no," he said. "I should turn you away." They locked eyes. Zane said nothing, despite the agony of waiting. Henry sighed and stepped away from the door. "Come in," he said.

—

Zane's mother read to him each night when he was a child, in both German and English. When Zane was nine, just six months before his mother's sedan would run off the road in the midst of a torrential downpour, he listened as she told him a fairytale about death.

This wasn't a story from one of his books, but one his mother's mother used to tell her in Germany, about a young girl who befriends death when death comes to take her grandfather away. They don't see each other again for another three years, until her dog dies, and death comforts her before departing once more. He takes her mother, her father, her husband (the now-woman argues here that the husband was too young, and she and death part ways bitterly until next time), her friends, until at last death comes for her, and she tells her family not to be sad, for she has waited a long time for this next adventure with her friend.

Zane used to be terrified of this story. Even at nine, he asked his mom why she continued to tell it. She held him closer and brushed his hair gently with her fingers. In German she told him, "Death is nothing to fear, Zane. Death is a natural part of life." She was adamant that the Nazis killed her parents, not death itself. He disagreed, but he didn't say anything. Instead, he asked her to tell him something nicer before he drifted off into dreams.

The accident that killed his mother was no one's fault. For Zane, that made everything even worse. To whom did he direct his rage? How could he cope with a true accident, with no parties to blame? In this way, his experience of his mother's and his wife's deaths had been vastly different. With Helena, there was a party at fault, a gunman framed as "unexpected" in his actions and "a tragedy" in his own right, despite a long list of previous anti-Semitic statements and a history of violence. Zane's younger self would have been surprised to learn it made him feel no better.

After Zane lost his wife, he couldn't help but be amazed that his mother's death hadn't left his father absolutely shattered. As a child, Zane was often embarrassed of his parents' affection. They kissed in front of his friends, held hands at school functions. His father could go on about his mother for hours. About the day they met. About how she was the reason he spoke German in the house. About how lucky he was to have found her.

It took Zane a little over a year after Helena's funeral before he could visit her grave a second time. He went on a chilly fall evening, wrapped in two jackets, a hat, and a scarf his mother made him a million years ago. The cold seeped into his bones regardless. He stripped off his knitted gloves and lay a hand on Helena's name, etched into the cold stone.

"I'm so lost without you," he told her, but Helena didn't answer. She was long gone.

Zane wouldn't remember the story about death and the girl until years later, until brainstorming tales to tell his own kids. He would miss his mother then, but it wasn't painful like it had been before. The story helped him recall her touch, gentle and reassuring, her smell, antiseptic from her job as a nurse and cinnamon-scented perfume. It helped him walk side by side with death and come to terms with its presence.

He told it to his kids the night after visiting Helena's grave for the second time, though he would tell it to them many times in the following years. Sometimes at night, sometimes in the middle of a random afternoon. Sometimes he would tell it to just the two of them and sometimes he would tell it when Lena's son Jason stayed over, when his cousin Rebecca asked him for a favor.

That night though, he gathered them in his arms and spoke until they fell asleep. He reveled in the feeling of them, heavy on his arms after they'd slipped away from him, into what he hoped to God were pleasant dreams.

—

It astounded Zane to see Miranda so open with someone so new to their lives. She insisted on sitting next to Henry at temple and Henry said he didn't mind. "She's great for my ego," he said, and Zane laughed.

They'd been together for a month the first time Henry asked Zane about coming with him to temple on a Saturday morning. "It means a lot to you," he said.

"It'll be boring," Zane hedged. Truly, he wasn't ready to bring Henry into the space that used to be his and Helena's. He never said as much, but Henry didn't push him.

In the meantime, Zane spent Saturday evenings with Henry, then weeknights too, and soon Henry spent most of his time at Zane's. Abby was still angry with him, but she was slowly coming around. It helped that she saw how much Zane was willing to do to make up for how he'd hurt Henry, going to doctor's appointments with him and combing over treatment plans.

It took another month before Zane asked Henry to go with him to synagogue, and Henry responded with a wide smile and kisses that left Zane breathless. He'd gone with them three times now, every week since the first. Noah had introduced him to everyone they could find and Miranda gave him a tour of the classrooms upstairs.

They rose for the Kaddish, and Zane snuck a glance at Henry out of the corner of his eye. Henry didn't know the words yet, but he stood in silence, eyes closed, respectful. He told Zane once that he thought about his parents during prayer, and Zane's mother, and Helena, and for now, that was more than enough for Zane.

Chapter Four: Hidden
1976-1993

In Lena's desperation to conceal herself from her pursuer, she nearly dove for the space under her grandparents' bed that wasn't occupied by old photo albums and boxes of junk. Just as quickly, she stopped herself. Under the bed was too obvious a hiding place. Everyone looked there first. Besides, there was always dust under there, always little balls of fuzz under her bare arms when she'd sought shelter there in the past. Lena shuddered and surveyed the rest of the upstairs for places to fit her slim eight-year-old body. She tugged at her dark hair and bit her lip.

Not downstairs. That's where *she* was, and *she* couldn't find her.

There! The laundry hamper, the one her grandmother said led straight down to the basement. Her grandmother threw clothes in there and they always disappeared into its depths. That's where she had to go if she wanted to escape.

Lena opened the lid. A long way down. She gritted her teeth, swallowing her fear, and put one leg over the side. An adult couldn't fit, but Lena easily threw her other leg over and lowered herself in from the lid of the hamper. She'd wiggled in almost entirely when she felt the snag on her hips, just large enough to get stuck at the base of the chute. Lena wrinkled her nose. Besides being a long drop, the cat hung out in the basement and it smelled of litter box and the decaying corpses of slaughtered mice.

Her head stuck dangerously out of the top of the hamper. *She* didn't know where Lena was yet, but Lena could hear her moving downstairs. Floorboards creaked as *she* moved from the kitchen to the living room, hunting. *She* would come upstairs soon enough and Lena couldn't be so exposed when that happened. She pushed against the sides of the shoot and tried to free her hips and felt her dress slide and her stomach drop and frantically grabbed for the lip of the chute.

Freedom! Her fingers poked out from over the top, but barely. That had to be enough.

She was upstairs. Lena heard her feet on the carpeted hallway, passing on her way to the bedrooms. Probably checking under the beds and in the closets. Lena smirked and mentally congratulated herself on her foresight.

Bathroom next. Lena heard the shower curtain slide against the rod. All in all, Lena had found a pretty fantastic hiding place. *She* hadn't thought of it at least.

Almost as soon as Lena heard her pursuer on the stairs, she realized just how sweaty her hands were. She readjusted her grip, but they slid regardless, like when she held on to a glass of ice water for too long. She had resolved to stay silent when she heard a *Bang!* in the basement.

A pipe? A rat? Another person? She didn't know. It didn't matter. Suddenly, falling into the unknown depths of her grandparents' house seemed a much worse fate than being caught.

"Claire!" she yelled. No answer. She took another breath and yelled, "Claire!"

She heard her sister's footsteps on the stairs again. "I'm in here! I'm in here!" The lid opened and Claire's pensive face appeared over the hamper's edge. Her thick eyebrows (a gift they'd both inherited from their mother's side of the family) flew into her hairline and her blue eyes (their father's side) widened.

"Get Grandma or Grandpa," Lena said. "Hurry!"

Claire's pensive face disappeared, and Lena struggled to hold on, breathing heavily. It took far too long, but Claire eventually came back with a red-faced Grandma, who pulled Lena out with strength Lena hadn't known she had. Grandma's arms were much too thin to have been able to lift an eight-year-old girl, her small body far too frail.

Apparently not.

"What were you thinking?" Grandma yelled as soon as Lena's feet found the floor. Her lips turned into an ugly scowl, her own thick, familial eyebrows deepening into a V. "What on earth made you climb in there?" Her German accent sharpened the words and made them daggers.

Lena refused to flinch, though she was properly abashed. "We were playing hide-and-seek," Lena said, studying her feet. They were rather dirty for someone who had just spent time in a laundry hamper. She stole a glance at Claire, likewise observing her blue and green striped socks. They wanted to play Secret Spies, the game Uncle Fred taught them, but apparently Grandma didn't like it when they played that one either. Grandma didn't like much.

"You could have died," Grandma said, holding her head in her hands.

Lena peered around Grandma, sneaking Claire a smile. "But I won," Lena said.

.

The alarm sounded and Lena groaned, painfully coming back into her twenty-year-old body. She smacked the clock and glared at Sid, snoring soundly beside her. He was the one who had to get up this early, and yet he never seemed to wake first.

Lena shook his arm. "Hey. Wake up." Her voice was rough with sleep. Her
head
throbbed
with last night's wine and cocaine. It had been such a good dream, a time in her life she had been too naive to realize she wasn't happy. There used to be moments, most of them with her sister, when she could pretend to be a normal girl living a normal life, not a victim or a failure.

After the laundry chute incident, Lena remembered, Grandma had sealed off the hamper with shiny silver duct tape. Lena and Claire didn't mind, though. It was no fun to play hide-and-seek after Lena found the best hiding place.

"Hmm." Sid rolled over and blinked. "S'morning?"

Lena ignored him and rolled over onto her side. She screwed her eyes shut and slipped back into uneasy dreams, no longer of childish games but of different parts of her childhood, far less pleasant.

.

Lena mostly lived at Sid's. He studied at the library most of the day, or went to class on campus, and Lena told him she went back to her three-bedroom, one-bathroom, six-roommate apartment during that time, but really she hung out at Sid's until whenever she had to go to work and came back after to do drugs and have sex. She didn't think he would mind, but she wanted to maintain some semblance of independence, even if that independence was fabricated.

Sid was a grad student at Columbia. Lena was a waitress. She had no illusions as to what their relationship really was. She spent the day in an apartment that wasn't hers, since Sid never came to her place (she wouldn't want him to anyway, so she never complained). She existed surrounded by photos of his family, people she had never met and never would meet. His parents, fresh off the plane from Calcutta, took up a prominent place on the mantel beside the TV. His two sisters sat in frames beside his undergrad degree on the wall of his office.

Some days, when Lena wasn't in the mood to feel quite so inadequate, she'd take the train from Manhattan to Long Island and visit her mom. Rebecca Rogers, a widow as of two years ago, refused to leave the home where she'd raised Lena and Claire, even though Lena refused to move back in and Claire had left for college not long ago.

Once upon a time, Lena, too, had college aspirations. She had attended a semester at NYU however many years ago, found herself in over her head, and promptly dropped out. Her mother claimed to understand. Lena had just lost her father after all. Lena nodded along and pretended like she'd ever given a shit about her dad. More recently, her mom had been not so subtly hinting that it might be time for Lena to ... how did she put it? "Return to her studies." Lena pretended to consider it in front of her mom and allowed herself to forget as soon as they parted ways.

On this particular day, Lena got off the train to her mom's and walked the twenty or so minutes from the station to the home she grew up in. Her

breath

quickened

as she walked up the drive, memories tightening her lungs in a vice-like grip. If Lena had it her way, her mother would have sold this house the moment her father died two years prior. There were no good memories at 157 Oakwood Drive. Nothing tied her mother to that address except sheer stubbornness and nostalgia for a misremembered past.

Her mom answered the door and gave her a quick hug. She asked if Lena would take a walk with her, to which Lena readily agreed. Less time indoors with old memories. She didn't need to see the room in which she had cried herself to sleep more nights than not, the living room in which she was brutally punished after Claire's Friday night service when Lena was fifteen. They walked down the old trail in the woods behind the house and Rebecca asked, "Have you heard from your sister recently?"

Lena shrugged. "Not really," she said. She and Claire were close as kids. They hadn't spoken much since Lena moved to the city two years before, first for NYU and then because it was better than living with her mother and her trauma. Her waitressing bills covered her rent, admission to her favorite clubs, and the occasional meal, though Sid often paid for both of the latter.

"She seems to enjoy school," Rebecca said. "It's good to hear her sounding happy."

"Hmm."

"Have you thought at all about returning to your studies?"

"I dunno." Lena kicked a rock down the path, where it tumbled into the grass and out of sight.

—

Lena loved her grandparents because she had to, but there wasn't much for a nine-year-old girl and her seven-year-old sister to do at their house, frankly, and she and Claire usually ended up watching cartoon tapes on their grandparents' old TV most of the time. That was, unless Uncle Fred came over with presents, which, to be fair, happened often enough. Uncle Fred wasn't actually her uncle, but a cousin of her mom or grandma, whoever. It didn't matter. His son, Zane, was twelve at the time and sullen. She supposed she could forgive him for it. His mom had died, like, two years ago after all. Even if she was frequently angry with her mother, she couldn't imagine growing up without her. Regardless, Lena preferred to stay out of his way and Zane probably didn't want to hang out with two little girls anyway.

It wasn't all bad. Grandpa Wally always called her "Buttercup" and hugged her close and that made her feel special and Grandma Gabi would slip her butterscotches and a wink when she wasn't yelling at her about the laundry chute, but Lena did miss her friends when she came up from Long Island to spend the weekend with Grandma and Grandpa.

Sometimes it wasn't even a weekend. Sometimes, like this time, they came up in the middle of the week for a holiday and she had to miss things like Todd Petre's and Karen Otubo's birthdays at school. Karen's birthday she didn't mind missing so much, since Karen always made fun of Lena for celebrating Hanukkah instead of Christmas and Karen's birthday wasn't actually until this weekend anyway, but she had a crush on

Todd and knew that if she wasn't there to give him a gift, he would notice one of the other girls in the class instead.

"It's an important holiday to celebrate with your grandparents," Lena's mom told her. Still, she didn't see why it had to be the same day as Todd's birthday.

The adults insisted on waiting for food, which Lena didn't understand, since she hadn't even fasted that day and she was still hungry. Uncle Fred even insisted on waiting until dinner before he gave her his present (probably ten dollars each), which was even worse. Lena always intended to save her gifts, but she often spent it the following week on chocolates and cookies from the store two streets over.

"Pst!" Lena turned around to where Claire was standing in the doorway of the kitchen. Her grandparents had separated the kitchen and the living room with a wall when Lena was three or four, though she didn't really remember how it was before.

Claire waved her over. "Lena," she whispered.

Lena glanced over at the adults, still deep in conversation. She came over to Claire in the kitchen and Claire led Lena to a drawer beside the sink. "What?"

"Look." Claire opened the drawer. It was papered with red poppies, but Lena could hardly see them under the junk. Bottle caps and batteries and buttons and thread. Claire opened the next drawer, where Lena frowned at the dozens of plastic and paper bags jammed into the small space.

"What—"

"I'm not done," Claire said, and she opened a third drawer, filled to the brim with hundreds of twist ties, maybe even thousands, white and blue and black. They lay on top of each other like Lena imagined bodies in a ditch would. They had just started World War II in school and it made her imagination run wild.

Lena scooped up a handful and examined them. "There are dates on here," Lena said. "This one is from 1946." This twist tie was older than her mother.

"I think 1948," Claire said, pointing to the last number. "That's an eight, not a six."

"Whatever," Lena said, scowling. Claire's eyes were better than hers. Lena would probably need glasses soon, but Todd Petre was more likely to kiss her if she wasn't wearing glasses. Plus, Karen would probably make fun of her even more.

"What are you doing?" Lena and Claire jumped, scattering handfuls of twist ties across the floor. Uncle Fred stood behind them, a glass of wine in his hand. The adults had broken out the food and drink, it seemed.

"Nothing," Lena and Claire said at the same time. Lena glared at her sister. Now they just looked suspicious.

Uncle Fred set the wine glass on the table and bent down to scoop up the scattered twist ties. His face remained impassive. Lena scrambled onto her knees to help him, followed by Claire. When they had finished putting the tiny bits of plastic back in the drawer, Uncle Fred said, "You found your grandmother's collection, huh?"

"Claire did," Lena said. This time, Claire glared at her.

"Ah. It's not nice to go through other people's things."

Lena stared down at her feet. "We're sorry," she said. Claire mumbled what might have been an apology too.

"Well, now you learned your lesson and you won't do it again," Uncle Fred said. He picked up his wine glass and said, "Now, who wants their holiday present?"

"Me, me, me!"

"I do, I do!"

Uncle Fred laughed and Lena followed him back into the dining room, where the grownups indulged in kugel and blintzes, the kind of food Lena only ever ate at her grandparents' house.

.

That was the last time Lena ever saw her Grandpa Wally. He died of a heart attack a week after whatever Jewish holiday they'd celebrated at his house. Later, Lena's mother would tell her she hadn't even known Grandpa Wally was sick.

"He died just like my sister," she told Lena. "His heart." Lena's mother rarely mentioned her sister. Lena often forgot she had one.

At the funeral, Grandma stayed huddled in a corner, away from the rest of the family. They sought out their Uncle Fred, who hugged Lena's mother tight, then turned to the children. Their father had gone outside to smoke with some of the men.

"Uncle Fred, do you have anything for us?" Claire asked.

"Claire, this is a funeral," their mother reprimanded, but Uncle Fredrick only smiled sadly.

"Not today, schatz." Not long after that, Lena's mother went to stand with her grandmother, and Lena and Claire spent most of the rest of the reception with Uncle Fred, who kept a running "who's who" of mourners for their benefit.

"That man used to work with your grandfather," he would say. "He gave him a job." Or, "That woman was a friend of your grandmothers from when she cleaned houses, when we came to America."

On the way home, Claire asked, "Uncle Fred is old. Is he going to die soon too?"

Their father nearly veered the car off the road. "Why would you say such a thing?" he bellowed. "Pay your uncle some respect." Claire burst into tears. Lena looked between Claire and her father and curled her knees up to her chest. They drove the rest of the way to the background noise of her mother's too-loud breathing and Claire's simpering sniffles.

—

Lena first met Sid at the diner. She was nineteen and serving Sid and his friends, a group of loud, self-aggrandizing students from the look of their Columbia sweaters. They were all older, grad students and law students and the like. She caught Sid's eye more than once, his lips curled into a smirk. He was cute, sure, but Lena didn't think anything of it until he left a generous tip and his number on the back of the receipt.

She didn't call him for a while. She was busy most nights, going out with her friends. The night she did call, Sid told her to pick a spot she liked. They met at The Red Room, a favorite bar of Lena and her friends. She was

hungover

and still a little drunk the morning (afternoon, rather) before her date. Once she'd managed to haul herself out of bed, she staggered over to the bathroom, threw up once into the toilet, brushed her teeth, and

did

a

line.

At the club, later, she and Sid joined with some of her friends in the graffiti-addled bathroom someone she knew claimed could give you an STD just from sitting on the toilet. As she bent over the sink to do another line, her friend Mindy stopped her. "Your nose is bleeding,"

Mindy said. Lena touched her hand to her face. It came away slick and red and sticky. She

laughed

and did the line. When she looked up, Sid was grinning at her. A touch of white powder dotted his own nose. She grinned back.

Lena had no memories of the first time she and Sid had sex, but she knew it was that night. She woke the next morning to Sid's alarm blaring in her ear. Her head

throbbed

and her thighs

ached

with whatever they'd done the night before. Since that first time, Sid had let her move some outfits to his apartment, some essentials. Her contact solution sat on the bathroom counter beside two toothbrushes and Sid's aftershave. He made it very clear that this was only for now, until he graduated in May, and that was fine by Lena. She had no desire to get attached.

—

The symptoms came on slowly. She was

nauseous

off and on, but that could have been the frequent hangovers. The

dizziness

too. She often felt unwell on her best days. It was only when a friend mentioned offhand how pregnancy made her head swim and her stomach swirl that Lena realized she hadn't gotten her period in three months.

It wasn't Lena's first pregnancy, although she was the only one who knew that. Lena met Tim Lambert, her friend Bianca's older brother, one night her sophomore year of high school at a party Bianca threw during her parent's monthly break from their children. Lena and Bianca were sophomores at the time, fifteen to Tim's twenty.

It was the night before Claire's Bat Mitzvah. The Friday night service had gone well, or as well as can be expected for a shy thirteen-year-old girl who'd cried the week before at the prospect of singing the prayers in front of half her school. Claire only faltered on the Hebrew twice, which Lena planned on teasing her for later, but she never got the chance. Their father cornered Lena at home (quite literally backed her into a corner) and gestured to her navy blue dress, lace wrapped in delicate patterns around the bodice. "You look like a

whore,"

he said. "What the hell were you thinking?" Behind her father, her mother stood, frozen, like she always did when Lena's father raged. Lena hated her for it. Claire, whose skirt came down to her knees, looked back and forth between them warily.

"I got this dress with Mom," Lena said. Her mother stiffened, and Lena felt a perverse sense of satisfaction. Good. Let her be afraid. This was her fault anyway.

Her father

slapped her. Lena's head

reeled. Her face

burned. Somewhere Lena couldn't see her, Claire cried out. "Dad!"

"Don't talk back to me," their father roared at Lena. He turned to Claire. "And you, you think you're grown now because you've had some wine with the rabbi." Claire cowered again. Their mom stood just a step behind her, eyes darting to the door.

That night, Lena snuck out the window of their one-story home to the white house with the red door down the street, where Bianca's party was in full swing. Bianca invited Lena in and handed her a beer and Lena spent most of the night flirting with Tim Lambert. By the time they had rushed sex in the closet of Tim's old bedroom, Lena could

barely

stand

upright,

her head reeling and her legs bucking at her knees. Tim held her up while he ravaged her neck.

Lena managed to sneak back into her room and make it through Claire's Saturday service the next morning without retching on the bima. All the while, she glared at her mother with mercifully unreddened eyes. Of course, her father was an asshole, but her mother didn't have to stay with him. Divorce wasn't nearly as taboo now as it had been in the dinosaur age, or whenever her parents grew up. Luckily, he hadn't left a bruise this time. She had no idea how she would've explained that to her friends. She eyed her grandmother and Uncle Fred in the congregation and wondered, for the first time, how much they knew.

Lena continued to sleep with Tim on weekends, on his college breaks. He slipped hints that there were other girls, but Lena told herself he was grandstanding. She was in love. Whether that was because he actually treated her well, or because he was older, or because he wasn't Jewish and that would piss off her parents, she didn't think about too much. She convinced herself he felt the same way, despite plenty of evidence to the contrary.

She was too young, too desperate, too broken to identify his need to control her as something other than overwhelming affection.

When Tim was home, he forbade Lena from seeing anyone else, even Bianca. When he called, she came. When he wasn't home, Lena wrote him at least two letters a week or he'd become suspicious. He rarely wrote her back. If her parents noticed her odd behavior, they didn't say anything. They broke up when Tim was expelled (she never did find out the reason) and joined the army.

Lena took a pregnancy test three weeks later, after three different teachers sent her to the nurse over the course of the week for painful nausea. She went to Planned Parenthood herself and told Claire she had a heavy period when she came back home with a bagful of pads and terrible stomach cramps.

Now, Lena went to her first OBGYN appointment since her abortion three years ago. The doctor congratulated her. No one had congratulated her the last time she'd seen a specialist for pregnancy. What a difference five years made.

"You're due in April," the doctor said. April. Right before Sid would graduate. Which meant she couldn't hide this from him. Lena thanked the doctor and left the building in a half-daze. Then she walked around to the back and cried until she was

gasping

for

air.

That night, lying in Sid's bed together, Lena brought up Sid's impending graduation. "Do you plan on staying in New York?" she asked. This was the first time they'd fucked while Lena was completely sober. She found it rather disappointing.

"I don't know," he said. "I have a couple prospects." Lena rolled her eyes in the dark at this pretentious almost-a-man she spent most of her time with and Sid continued, "Why do you ask?"

Lena shrugged, her shoulder coming up against Sid's. "Just wondering," she said. Not that Sid would object to continuing in their relationship if he did stay, not until he found someone he could actually love.

"Ok." Sid reached over and put a hand on her breast, stroking it gently, and Lena turned away.

"I'm tired," she said.

.

The mothers in her family had always let their children down. Her grandmother, who'd pit her two children against each other and forced her daughter into an abusive marriage, though no one else seemed to see it that way. Her mother, who stayed in that marriage until Silas Rogers died young and not so tragically. Lena knew nothing of the mothers before that, the woman who raised her grandmother and all the women that came before that, but given the two data points she had, a second abortion was an easy decision, or so she thought until she made the appointment.

Almost immediately after she hung up with Planned Parenthood, Lena set a hand on her still-flat stomach, stood up suddenly, and immediately sat down again as a wave of
dizziness
nearly knocked her over. Freaking pregnancy hormones. Lena breathed deeply and stood again, slower this time. She went to Sid's phone and redialed the number she had stored in her bag but that she had since memorized purely by staring at it for so

long. The phone rang and then a voice at the other end said, "This is Liliana at Planned Parenthood. How can we help you?"

Not the person she'd just spoken to. For the best. That would have embarrassed her so much she might have hung up.

"Hi. Um. I have an appointment for next week for an abortion. I'd like to cancel it." Lena gripped the phone so hard her hand turned white. She felt her stomach again under her palm. How long before she felt the little person growing inside her?

"Sure, not a problem. What's the first and last name?"

Perhaps she could have simply skipped the appointment, but too late now. "Lena Rogers," she said, stumbling slightly over her own name. "It's for the fourteenth at three."

"I see it. No problem, Lena, you're all set. If you need anything else, please feel free to contact us."

Lena thanked the person on the other end, hung up the phone, and took a deep breath. She could do this. She would be better than they were. She would

break

the cycle.

As she packed, she wondered how on earth the few possessions she had at Sid's apartment had scattered so much in such a short time. Her clothes lay haphazardly at the bottom of his closet, her coat rested where she'd flung it over the back of his chair. She threw on her jacket, shoved her shirts and pants into her bag, and tucked her contact solution and earrings into the front pocket. With one final look back at the family photos that weren't hers in an apartment where she'd never truly felt comfortable, Lena left.

—

Lena was twelve the year she realized how fucked her family really was. They took a trip to Jamaica for the Christmas holiday, since Hanukkah that year had fallen in earlier December. As soon as they stepped out of the airport, the sticky heat suffocated her from all sides, even though she wore just a tank top and shorts. All of them wore similar outfits. They'd been quite a sight when they arrived at the Newark airport in December, but now they blended right in.

Her dad hefted his bag over his shoulder and turned to her mom. "Guess we gotta look for that shuttle," he said.

Claire pointed at the sign over their heads. *Shuttle to Marriott,* it read. Lena's dad led the way, followed by Lena and Claire, then their mom. Lena's mom had been hesitant about coming to Jamaica for Christmas, if for no other reason than that they had never done it before. A blue Christmas instead of a white one, not that it mattered to them. They rarely traveled and Lena wasn't sure her mom had ever been out of the country before, but her mom hadn't said anything to Lena's dad other than to timidly suggest they visit his parents in Florida or that they travel to Israel for the holiday season if they were to travel at all, even though she'd never been there either. So here they all were, on this barely concealed parody of a happy family vacation, because Lena's mom didn't have a damn spine.

Like always, her mom carried only one backpack. She had always been a light packer, but neither Lena nor Claire could never quite master the art of folding things so they actually fit in their bags. Their mother had to do it for them. The shuttle pulled up and a handful of tourists descended with their luggage, but it was only Lena's family who got on. They loaded their bags onto the luggage rack and sat, Lena and Claire side by side across from their parents, neither of them reaching for the other.

Just take her hand, Lena thought, looking back and forth between them, but it was like watching strangers on this bus, like Lena was alone but for a random pair of tourists across from her, a young girl (who happened to look strikingly like her) to her right, the bus driver, and four bags of luggage. Had her parents ever been happy? They must have been, or they wouldn't have married. Her father must have been charming, her mother bolder. It was this moment, watching her parents decidedly fail to interact, that she realized how
  broken
  her family was. In that moment, staring across the bus at the two people she was supposed to trust more than anyone else in the world, she felt so deeply the
  fractures
  between
  them
  all.

—

Uncle Fred's Brooklyn home was much more colorful than Lena remembered from the last time she was there. The walls were a baby blue and the couch a vibrant lilac. The kitchen, to the right of the entrance and across from the coat closet, had reddish-pink granite countertops. The near-forest at the back door boasted two large, red flowers with vibrant yellow centers and, of course, a variety of greenery undoubtedly left over from her late Aunt Nina, her uncle's wife until she died in a car accident when Lena was only four. Lena remembered little of her aunt, but she did remember the garden her aunt kept in the back yard, the way she nearly always had soil under her unpainted finger nails. The flora and their vibrancy should have been beautiful, but in Lena's current state of contradictory panic

and

numbness,

just looking around hurt her head. "You ok?" Uncle Fred asked.

Lena realized he'd been standing in his entryway now for nearly a minute. "Yeah," she lied. She raised her right hand from her still-flat stomach and clutched the strap of her backpack. All she had was that and the duffle in her left.

She had been clearing her things out of her overcrowded apartment downtown when she realized she had nowhere to go. Not her mom's. If the stress of living there didn't kill the life growing inside her, the alcohol she'd have to consume to get through it surely would. Her grandmother would freak. Her uncle, though, had always been good to her. Zane was older now and living with his girlfriend at a picturesque house in suburban Westchester, so it was just Lena and Uncle Fred.

He put a hand on Lena's arm, and Lena tried not to flinch. "Why don't you unpack," Uncle Fred said. "I'll make something to eat."

"Sure," Lena said, even though she wasn't hungry and even though she didn't have very many belongings to unpack in the first place.

Uncle Fred gestured to the hallway, down which Lena would find the guest room. Zane's old room. "There are more blankets in the closet if you need them."

"Thank you," Lena said, even though she already knew that. She slipped into the spare room before Uncle Fred could ask what she wanted for lunch.

The sheets were a bright maroon, but the rest of the room was more muted, tans and browns on the walls and floor. Though he didn't live here any longer, much of the room screamed Zane. His old books sat on a tall, white bookshelf in the corner of the room. Fantasy and science-fiction sat prominently on the top shelf, schoolbooks by the likes of long-dead white men Lena didn't know placed toward the bottom. On the top of the bookshelf lay Zane's undergrad degree and a cardboard box of knickknacks. A poorly formed ceramic bowl Zane had clearly made himself as a child and an old playbill from *The Sound of Music* sat half-concealing the latter books on the lower shelf.

On the dresser, a photo of Zane and his girlfriend, Zane's arms around Helena's shoulders, sat in a place of honor beside the mirror opposite the headboard. On the other side of the dresser was a photo of Zane and his parents, all dressed up for an event Lena either couldn't remember or hadn't attended. Zane must have been eight or nine when this photo was taken, giving Aunt Nina no more than a year or two left to live.

Lena set both bags on her temporary bed and glanced at the mirror. She was all

out

of

sorts, her hair uncombed and greasy, her cheeks hollow and nearly white. The collar of her shirt had shifted slightly out of place, just enough to notice. She tugged it back over her collarbone.

Back in the kitchen, Lena smelled something spiced and warm. Uncle Fred looked up from the stove and smiled. "Lunch should be ready in ten minutes," he said. "You can use the bathroom on the hall. I've got everything you need under the sink."

"Ok."

"How are you feeling?" Uncle Fred asked. He put his spatula aside and faced Lena. "Really."

"I'm ok," Lena said softly, sitting on the kitchen counter. "Thank you for letting me stay. However I can help out around here or, I don't know."

"Hush," Uncle Fred said, picking up the spatula again. "You're family, schatz."

Not for the first time in her life, Lena wished she'd grown up with Uncle Fred.

Eventually, of course, Lena's stomach grew to the point where she could no longer hide her pregnancy from one Rebecca Rogers. Uncle Fred sat with Lena and her mom at her mom's place and Lena told her everything. Tears pooled in her mom's eyes, and Lena looked away.

"You're so young," her mom said.

"You were my age when you had me," Lena said. She was too freaking tired for this. The night before, between the nauseating discomfort in her stomach and her anxiety over confronting her mother, she'd gotten maybe three hours of sleep.

"It was different," her mom insisted. "I had a partner."

Lena pressed her lips together to keep herself from yelling. She'd rather have no partner than a man who hit her kid. It astounded her that her mom still disagreed after all these years.

God, she missed alcohol. What she wouldn't do for a glass of wine.

"Right now," Uncle Fred said, "Lena really needs our support."

Lena's mom looked as though she hadn't quite decided between crying or yelling. "Of course I'll support her," she said. "Do you know if it's going to be a boy or a girl?" Her voice quivered.

"No." They avoided each other's eyes. What else was there to say?

"We'll get you set up," Uncle Fred said. "We can all pitch in with babysitting too."

"Ok." Lena stared down at her well-worn sneakers.

"Are you sure you can do this?" her mom asked.

Yes. She should say yes. She should reassure her mother, reinforce her uncle's trust in her, but she didn't know at all. She had no blueprint for what it was like to be a good mother. Her hand drifted to her stomach, as it did so often these past few months.

No, she hadn't meant to get pregnant, but she wanted this child. This child would know they were wanted, so help her. But she didn't know what came next, what it meant to be a mother and to love her baby unconditionally. So when Lena's mother asked if she could do this, Lena at last looked her mother in the eye and said, "I don't know."

.

When they arrived home, Uncle Fred insisted on making them both hot chocolates. They sat in the living room, on the lilac couch, not talking for a moment. Her nausea had dissipated and Lena's stomach felt

empty,

hollow,

despite the life growing inside of it. Was it so wrong to want to prove she could do this on her own? Was that a horrible reason to become a mother? It had to be better than her own parents' reason. She bit her lip to stem the sudden onslaught of tears fighting to escape at the memory of her conversation with her father, information she never should have known, and mentally cursed her hormones once more. Why couldn't pregnancy make her inexplainably joyful instead of ready to scream at any moment?

Uncle Fred sipped his drink and wiped his mouth on the back of his hand. "I feel like we failed you," he said. Lena raised her eyebrows but didn't say anything. Her uncle continued, "You shouldn't have to do this alone, Lena. You should have had a different kind of life."

Lena cleared her throat. "I made my own choices," she said softly. The last thing she wanted was for Uncle Fred to blame himself. Actually, the last thing she wanted was to think her choices were at all dictated by her parents or even Uncle Fred. And yet, it was true that Lena had failed in her mother's eyes, becoming an unwed and uneducated mother just out of her teens, and Rebecca had failed in Lena's.

"Maybe," he said, nodding. "I wonder if we can ever escape the shadows of those who came before us."

Lena sipped her drink slowly. "We'll be ok, Uncle Fred." We. She hadn't meant to say *we*. She put a hand on her stomach self-consciously. Still, she felt nothing under the bulge in her sweater. Perhaps she should ask the doctor about that.

Uncle Fred peered into his mug and Lena finished the rest of her hot chocolate. "I'm going to lie down," she said. "Thank you for everything."

"Of course," her uncle said. "I love you, Lena."

Lena gave him a soft smile. She didn't deserve his kindness, not after all the ways she had messed up. Like she said, she made her own choices, and now Uncle Fred had to suffer for them. "Love you too," she said before disappearing into her cousin's old room for the night. She lay on the bed and waited for sleep to come, early as it was.

She pressed a gentle hand to her stomach. "We will be ok," she whispered. "I promise I won't let anything bad happen to you."

She felt a flutter in response. Lena gasped quietly and pressed a little harder. The sensation deepened, the life inside her communicating in the only way it knew how. Lena couldn't help but smile, her eyes filling again. "We'll be ok," she repeated, stroking her stomach carefully. "We'll be ok."

—

A few years ago, toward the end of his life, Lena went into the hospital to see her father on her own. The cancer had taken his sight already, exchanged it for frequent migraines and crushing body aches. Today was an ok pain day, but he didn't seem to know where he was, or who Lena was. He kept talking to her as though he thought she was her mother.

She wasn't sure why she'd come except that her mother had asked her to, over and over. Lena had refused for weeks until her mom broke down in tears and asked Lena why she wouldn't do this one thing for her. Claire, then a high-school sophomore, went to see their dad almost every day, which her mom mentioned constantly, though Claire never made Lena feel bad over it. In fact, Lena and Claire never talked about it at all.

In the few weeks since Lena had seen her father last, he'd become an entirely different person. Dark stubble littered his normally smooth cheeks. His whole face was thinner, skeletal. His deep blue eyes had cooled, lightened almost, and stared at nothing. The whites had gone the color of faded dog urine. Lena eyed his bony hand and wondered if she should take it.

"I'm so scared," he rasped. "My parents, they need me." Lena didn't say anything, so he went on. "My buddy John, he was drafted. He died in the field, Rebecca. He died." It took her a second to realize he was talking about the Vietnam War, the war she and Claire had both been born into. Her dad hadn't fought, as far as she knew. She never knew why.

"I'm sorry," Lena murmured. What else could she say? Any chance her father had to make things right had gone with his sanity.

"We need to have a baby," her dad said. "If we have a baby, they can't send me away. I can stay here with you."

Lena's stomach lurched. "A

baby?"

Her dad smiled at her. His teeth had yellowed from a lack of frequent brushing. "That's right," he said. "A baby, and we'll be together. Isn't that what you want?"

She never asked her mom about this sham of a conversation, but she knew what it meant. Had her mother even wanted her? Had anyone? She had been born a tool to keep her father safe, destiny pre-determined, and no one had been sure of what to do with her when that destiny, upon her conception, had been fulfilled. She had no purpose now.

Lena never told Claire what she knew either. Something had fractured between them that day, the day Lena learned her origins, and she couldn't bring herself to pass that burden onto Claire, the dutiful daughter. Claire, who every day visited the man who'd made their lives a living hell. Claire, whom the knowledge surely would have broken, whether their parents' choices then had led to one unwanted child or two.

In so many ways, Lena had failed to protect her sister. She could carry this one burden alone.

—

Later, many years later, when Lena's son was five and Lena was using

again, Claire came by for a visit. Lena opened the door and frowned at her unexpected visitor. "What are you doing here?"

"Hello to you too." Claire surveyed Lena from head to toe, and Lena bristled. Her hair was unbrushed at best, nest-like at worst. She'd lost too much weight in the last few weeks and her unwashed Rolling Stones T-shirt hung loosely around her overstretched frame. Her collar bone
jutted
out from under her skin. She
squinted
in the morning light, in part because she was hung over, in part because she hadn't had the energy to put her contacts in this morning and her glasses were at least four years out of date.

"Mom was worried about you," Claire admitted.

"She could have come here herself."

"You know how she is," Claire said, smoothing a hand over her pleated skirt. Her own hair was tied back into a tight bun.

Lena did indeed. Their mother never wanted to talk about anything hard. Her drug addict-slash-alcoholic daughter
using
again, among other things, most definitely qualified as something hard. "Come in," Lena said at last.

Claire followed her into the toy-strewn house and sat across from Lena at the dining table. She laid her arm on the table. Took it off again. "Where's Jason?"

"School," Lena said. "It's a Tuesday."

"Oh wow, I didn't realize he'd started kindergarten already."

"I mean, yeah," Lena said. "That's how time works."

"He's so big," Claire said, grinning at the photo behind Lena. It was a picture of Jason on his first day of school, his denim backpack almost as big as his torso. He grinned widely up at the camera, his head angled to the left. He looked remarkably like

the man Lena had shared a bed with all those years ago, eyes bright and dimples prominent on his little face. Lena's mother had taken the picture. She'd shown up that day claiming she and Lena had talked about it over the phone. They probably had, to be fair. Lena
didn't
remember.

"Have you gotten enough to satisfy Mom yet?" Lena asked.

"It's not about Mom," Claire said. "What can I do for you?"

Lena laughed, but it was
hollow. It made her chest
hurt. She realized she was close to tears. "I
can't
be
helped."

Claire pursed her lips, and for a moment, she could have been their mother's twin. They all used to look so alike, until Lena had let herself become a wasted shell of the woman she used to be. "C'mon, Lena."

As a child, Claire had looked up to her, even told Lena once when she was six or seven that she wanted to be just like her.

"I'm a shit show," Lena said.

"After everything we went through?" Claire asked. "Yeah, I think you're pretty well adjusted."

"Ha. You're going to law school Claire. I'm a twenty-five-year-old single mother and a drug addict and you're going to law school."

"Would you consider rehab?" Claire asked.

A total dodge, but whatever. Lena shook her head. "They
can't
help
me."

"Look," Claire said, "I get that you have to hit rock bottom or whatever but—"

"You don't 'get' anything," she said sharply. Claire had been the victim of just as many beatings, just as many verbal attacks, just as much trauma, and yet she hadn't gone off the deep end. She didn't start
shaking
every time she stepped foot in their mother's house. She was so normal it
hurt.

"Ok, fine," Claire snapped. "You know what I don't get? I don't get how you could be all high and mighty claiming you're going to do better than mom and then keep cocaine in the same house as your five-year-old son. I don't get how you won't accept that she was abused too. I don't get how you can go on and on about me and my perfect life when you left
me
alone."

The air between them stilled. "What the hell are you talking about?" Lena asked, even though she wasn't sure she wanted to know the answer.

"You went to college and you *left*," she said. "I needed you."
oh god her head spun
"Dad had just died and Mom didn't know what to do and you decided you'd rather be strung out every night
where was the alcohol
than check in every once in a while. So fuck you, Lena."

Her words stung worse than any blow their father could have landed. "That's not
I can't do this I can't I can't
fair," Lena insisted.

"Isn't it? I've always been there for you and Mom. Always. You got to fuck around and make mistakes and if I did that too? It would have
broken
her."

"Who gives a shit?" Lena howled. "We were already broken, Claire."

"All right," Claire said, standing. "All right. Good fucking luck. If you ever get your shit together, feel free to call." She stormed out, and Lena didn't bother chasing after her.

The door shut and slowly, Lena rose from her seat. She went into the kitchen and grabbed the wine from the
cabinet beside the fridge. She uncapped it and took a long,
slow
drink. When she thought she'd be sick from it, she at last set it down and wiped her mouth with the back of a
shaking hand. It came away somewhere between violet and
blood
red.

.

That night, after she tucked Jason in
(or maybe she didn't),
Lena had the same recurring dream of the same childhood memory she'd had for years, of her and Claire playing hide-and-seek in her grandparents' house. Stuck in the laundry chute that led to the unknown depths of her grandparents' basement, she shouted for Claire. "I'm in here!" she cried. "I'm in here!"

Her sister's face peered over the edge, six-years-old and frighteningly innocent. Lena gripped the edge of the chute, panting, and Claire returned with their grandmother, who pulled Lena out of the chute and from certain death (or at least injury) with everything she possessed, adrenaline granting her twig-like limbs with strength she shouldn't have possessed.

"What were you thinking?" Grandma howled. "What on earth made you climb in there?"

"We were playing hide-and-seek," Lena told her. She wasn't thinking. It was so much *easier* not to think.

Grandma put her head in her hands. "You could have died," she said.

Lena pushed a toe against the cream carpet. She forced herself to meet her grandmother's angry stare and for the first time in her short life, Lena wondered what her grandmother was so afraid of.

She held her grandmother's gaze and slowly, she began to smile as she said, "But I won."

Chapter Five: Left of Yesterday
1958-1997

The best thing in the world was ice cream, or so Rebecca thought when she was ten years old. She delighted in walking hand in hand with her father and licking strawberry cream from a sugar-spun cone. On this particular day, they had gone to the new store several blocks over to get the fancy kind with real strawberries in it. At least, they looked real. It didn't matter much to Rebecca, as they were delicious. Her dad had gotten chocolate, with dark pieces hidden in the cream.

"What say you we walk to water?" her dad said in English. His German was much better than his English, but Rebecca didn't know German well and he often insisted on speaking in English anyway, even to people who spoke German too, like his coworkers or Rebecca's mom. All the German Rebecca knew, she had picked up from listening to her parents speak to each other in short bursts of the language, or to Uncle Fredrick. Uncle Fredrick's English was perfect, though, and he almost never spoke German back.

Rebecca nodded and licked the thick cream dripping pink rivers down the sides of her cone. She tugged on her father's hand and they walked from the ice cream shop to the water under the Brooklyn Bridge. Her friends said the neighborhood was called DUMBO and that it stood for something, but the only image she could think of when someone said "Dumbo" was the elephant with the big ears from the Disney movie. The bits with Dumbo's mom almost always made Rebecca's younger sister Ellie cry.

When Ellie was born, the whole family used to come down to the water together. Mom would pack a picnic and Dad would carry Ellie in his arms and Rebecca would ride on his back. When the doctor diagnosed Ellie with a heart problem two years ago, though, she stopped coming down to the water with them, since Mom said she couldn't walk that far on her own, though she never explained what would happen if they tried. Mom stayed behind with Ellie now while Rebecca walked to the water with Dad or went to the grocery store with her uncle. Besides, even if she longed for the days before her sister's diagnosis, Rebecca and Ellie were both too big now for Dad to carry them.

When Rebecca came home with Dad, Ellie grinned up at them from her position at the kitchen table and held up a sheet of paper, ink aligned in two straight rows down the page.

"I got all the math right," she said.

Rebecca came closer and saw that the paper was full of plus and minus signs, and even a multiplication problem or two. Rebecca was pretty sure she hadn't studied multiplication until this year, but Ellie may have asked her teacher for the problems. She did that often, as bored as she was with the problems they'd been assigned. The other kids teased her and told her she was a teacher's pet. Rebecca had confronted more than one of Ellie's bullies on the playground.

"She is a genius," Mom said, kissing Ellie on the head. "Now, why you no go play with your sister, hmm?"

Ellie looked up at Rebecca, batting her eyelashes.

"All right," Rebecca said. She'd wanted to phone her friends, perhaps go to Ginny or Tess's house in the evening, but she had never been able to say no to Ellie. Rebecca took her hand and they went over to the living room corner where they'd last left their dolls, Raggedy Ann and Barbie. Rebecca preferred Raggedy Ann, but she let Ellie use her first anyway.

That night, lying in their twin beds in the room they shared, Ellie called her name quietly in the dark. "Becca?"

"Hmm?" Rebecca rolled over until she faced the other side of the room, where Ellie was supposed to be asleep. Ellie was the only one who called her Becca. Mom and Dad always called her Rebecca, and Ginny and Tess and the rest of her friends at school called her Bex. Becca was special, just for her sister.

"Am I going to die?"

Rebecca pushed herself up onto her elbows. "Why do you think that?" She could just make out Ellie's dark outline on the bed, huddled up by her pillow.

"I heard Mom talking to Uncle Fred," she said. "Mom was crying. And she said ..." Ellie closed her eyes, trying to remember, then presumably translate the conversation into English. Like with everything else, Ellie was better at languages than Rebecca, but she still wasn't anywhere near fluent. "She said that she didn't want me to die like Erika and Eli. She was wondering if she had cursed me with my name."

"Who's Erika?" Rebecca asked. They both knew Eli from the stories, mostly Uncle Fredrick's stories. He was Mom's brother from before Uncle Fredrick and he still lived in Germany, but they didn't know why they could never see him. The concept of a brother before Uncle Fredrick confused Rebecca and Ellie both, so amongst themselves they just said Mom had two brothers.

Ellie shrugged in the dark. "She told Uncle Fred I have a weak heart."

"But we know that already."

"Yeah."

"And you're not dead yet." Rebecca paused, then added, "And you won't be if I can help it." It was a ridiculous thing to say, but she had to say something to reassure her frightened sister.

Ellie giggled and Rebecca smiled in spite of herself. "Yeah," Ellie said, "you'll protect me." She slurred on the last word, her voice suddenly heavy with sleep, and rolled over so that she was facing the wall. "G'night, Becca."

"Goodnight." She had barely gotten the word out when Rebecca heard Ellie's soft snores from the other side of the room. Delicate. Breakable. They both knew about Ellie's "condition," as Mom referred to it, but Rebecca tried not to think about it too much. Nothing would happen to Ellie. She was too young for death, too kind for death. Besides, she never got sick, even with colds. She never *acted* sick, except sometimes she got tired easily or ran out of breath.

Rebecca rolled over and stared at the opposite wall, but it was a long time before she fell asleep again. She dreamed that she was a knight from a story book, off to save Princess Ellie from a raging dragon they all called Heart.

.

Rebecca found the book in her mother's closet that weekend, playing dress up with her clothes with Ellie. "*Max und Moritz*," she read aloud. Rebecca knew enough German to know that "und" meant "and," and also to translate some of the next part. *"Eine Bubengeschichte in sieben Streichen."* A Book of Seven ... Seven what?

"Oh, that looks old," Ellie said. "Do you think that was Mom or Dad's?"

It *did* look old. The hardcover was torn in two places, small white scratches around the edges. Several of the pages stuck out between the others, indicating that they'd likely come loose in the last however many years. The cover was dingy and graying, the ink that made up the two small characters on the cover faded with time.

"Maybe," Rebecca said, and she opened the book, glad to have a distraction anyway. She was too old for dress up, really, but Ellie had wanted to play. Ellie practically swam in a purple overcoat and a pleated yellow skirt. Rebecca wore the tailored tweed dress she almost always chose among Mom's things.

In loopy handwriting on a blank front page of the mysterious book, someone had scrawled, *An Franklin, ich hoffe, es gefällt euch. Alles Liebe, Anna,* in blue pen. Didn't liebe mean love? It wasn't Mom's then, and Mom and Dad didn't know anyone named Franklin or Anna. Or, Rebecca didn't think they knew anyone with those names. She knew very little of their lives before she and Ellie existed.

The girls turned to the first page, but before they could start translating, Mom appeared in the doorway, an apron tied around her waist and a spatula in her hand. "What are you doing?" she yelled. "Close it." Her face swelled with rage and a vein in her forehead throbbed.

Rebecca snapped the book shut and held it out to Mom. Ellie's lip quivered.

Mom snatched the book from Rebecca so hard the edge smacked her hand. Rebecca's eyes watered, but she didn't cry. Mom stuffed it under a pile of shirts on the top shelf, out of Rebecca's reach and shouted, "Go play in your room."

"Ok," Rebecca said softly. "Sorry." She wasn't quite sure what she was sorry *for*, but she knew she never wanted to make Mom angry like that. She took Ellie by the hand and led her back to their bedroom. Ellie sniffed to herself until Rebecca took a random Dr. Seuss book from the shelf and began to read it out loud, even though Ellie was far too smart for kids stories. The two of them curled up on Rebecca's bed together. By the time Rebecca finished the book, Ellie had tucked herself under Rebecca's arm, snuggled close to her side. She asked Rebecca to read it again, and Rebecca flipped to page one.

—

Years later, at Ellie's funeral, Rebecca recalled these memories as her parents sobbed through the whole service, leaving no room for Rebecca's grief. Not the specifics of the memories, per se. She couldn't remember what Ellie wore from their mother's closet playing dress up, for instance, or the conversation they'd had the night Rebecca had falsely and childishly reassured Ellie she'd protect her from death, but she remembered what it was like to love her sister. She remembered the joy in Ellie's eyes when they played together, the pride bursting from Rebecca's chest when Ellie ran to her for comfort instead of to their mother.

Her parents were too distraught to address the small crowd and Rebecca didn't know what she could possibly say to capture the Ellie she knew, the young girl who used to sit on the edge of her lap and listen to her stories. Ellie, who used to wake her in the middle of the night to chase away the bad dreams, holding a stuffed Roo from the Winnie-the-Pooh books. Ellie, who was supposed to be the first in their family to go to college. Ellie, on whom all their parents' hopes for this country had rested. Uncle Fred addressed the mourners instead, saying things like "brilliant" and "engaging" and "gone too soon." Ellie had been all of those things, but she had also been so much more.

Rebecca didn't know at least half the people who came up to her at Ellie's Shiva. Her parents and Uncle Fred and his wife and son were all there, of course, and Tess and Ginny both made an appearance, but so did kids Rebecca had never met from Ellie's class in school. She saw several young women from the temple she thought she might know in context, but not here. A cluster of young, unfamiliar men introduced themselves to Rebecca and Dad. They said they were there when Ellie died and wanted to pay their respects. Rebecca remembered there being young men roughly her and Ellie's age that day by the water, but she didn't know their faces. She pretended to recognize them and thanked them for their condolences when Dad was too over-come with grief to do so.

Mom came and sat beside her after an hour or so. She wore sunglasses even though they were inside. They didn't hide the tear tracks over her too-red cheeks. Rebecca spoke first. "She would have hated this," she said.

Mom nodded. "She would have cried," she said. "She always cried." Mom's voice came out soft, nasal. Rebecca couldn't recall a single time in the past few days that her parents hadn't been red-faced and congested.

"We went and saw *The Parent Trap* last summer," Rebecca said. "She cried the whole second act. It wasn't a sad movie."

Mom turned to Rebecca. "Thank you," Mom said. "For trying to save her."

Rebecca should have been grateful for the acknowledgment. Instead, it rankled. What would she have done instead? Mom and Dad weren't the only ones who loved Ellie, but so often they very nearly forgot they had an older daughter who cared for Ellie just as much as they did, who'd been there for Ellie when neither of them could be.

Nothing Rebecca ever did seemed good enough for her them, not unless it had to do with Ellie, taking care of Ellie, saving Ellie, and even then, she couldn't compare. Not when they had a better, smarter daughter, a daughter they could have pinned their futures on, a daughter who could never do wrong again when Rebecca had so many opportunities.

No, that wasn't fair. She took that last thought back.

.

Death loomed over Rebecca's life. The death of her mother's family in the German internment camps so many years before she was born still somehow resonated all the way down to Rebecca. Ellie, her sister and her best friend, gone in, ironically, the span of a heartbeat. Their uncle's wife, also far too young, though not a teenager. A car wreck, sudden, killed by a brutal winter storm and a dysfunctional break. By that funeral, Rebecca had two daughters of her own. It was Lena and Claire's first, Rebecca's second.

Again, Uncle Fred took to the front of the room, using words like "lively" and "generous" and "beloved." Words that described the woman Rebecca knew well enough, but he couldn't quite capture how witty Aunt Nina had been, how sharp. He couldn't explain in the words allotted how, when Lena fell on the driveway, once, Aunt Nina sang to her until she stopped crying, or how, whenever they all got together during Rebecca's childhood, she made Rebecca and Ellie and even Mom laugh and laugh for hours.

Uncle Fred delivered his speech in a monotone, void of all emotion, far from the delighted, loving voice he'd used with his wife when she'd lived. Rebecca glanced at Zane, Uncle Fred and Aunt Nina's ten-year-old son, around her children. Zane sat with fists clenched, in the front row of the temple, staring at his father without seeing him. She wanted to comfort this child whose grief had already eaten at him so completely, and somehow, Rebecca didn't know what to tell him. It never got better, not really. There were times in the years since Ellie's death when Rebecca very nearly felt joy again, like she could finally move on and into a life not consumed by anguish and nostalgia for what was, only to be overwhelmed by loss on an anniversary, Ellie's birthday or her date of death, and the hopelessness invaded the Ellie-shaped cavity in her chest all over again.

Rebecca's father died mere years after Aunt Nina's funeral. By the time he passed, Rebecca was all grown up, in her early thirties. It upended her world all the same.

At Dad's funeral, Rebecca left her children with Uncle Fred and went to visit her mother, again standing alone in the corner of the room, despite the abundance of friends, of family, of colleagues there to offer condolences. She and Mom stood side by side in a long stretch of silence before Mom asked, "Did your father ever tell you how we met?" Rebecca shook her head and Mom continued, "We were at school together. Kindergarten. I asked him to marry me the first week, and he said, 'Ok.'" Mom shrugged slightly when she said, "Ok," and Rebecca pictured her father doing it, but as he was before he died. Rebecca had no pictures of her father as a young boy. Not of him, nor of her mother, nor of Uncle Fredrick. They hadn't taken any from Germany when they fled. Her Aunt Nina had kept a handful from her own childhood, stolen away last-minute and stored under piles of clothing on her journey to the States, that she had treasured beyond measure. She wondered where those photos were now.

Mom glanced up and gave Rebecca a small smile. "I married him that year on the playground," she said.

"You married him?" Rebecca asked with a small smile of her own. She had never thought of her mother as a bold woman, but she supposed Mom might have been an entirely different person in Germany, someone who could have been sponta- neous and carefree. It was a sad thought. The war had killed millions, but it had done just as much damage to those left living.

—

If one of them had to go to university, Rebecca knew it should be Ellie. Still, she couldn't help it that her stomach gave a little lurch when she remembered she wouldn't be the one granted such an opportunity, that her mouth turned down at the corners when she saw fifteen-year-old Ellie studying in the kitchen for the tests she would soon take. When Rebecca graduated next year, she'd never go to school again.

For now though, it was summer. The girls snuck out of the house with their bathing suits and sunglasses to sit by the water, a walk Ellie hadn't done since she was little. "Even then, I think I could have made it here without having a literal heart attack," Ellie said, stretching her towel out on the side of the river. "I was never *that* sick." Several boys their age tossed a Frisbee nearby. By the water, a group of children played with toy boats.

"You know Mom," Rebecca said. Perhaps they'd stop for ice cream on the way back. Ellie would like that. Rebecca would like that, come to think of it. She hadn't had ice cream since last summer, at least.

"Hey," Ellie said, putting a hand on Rebecca's shoulder. "I am sorry. That you can't go to school."

Rebecca bit her lip, but quickly arranged her face in a smile when she looked at Ellie. "You never know. You'll just have to make a lot of money and pay for me to go later."

Ellie laughed, tipping her head back. One of the boys glanced over at them. At Ellie, rather. He surveyed her wavy hair, tied back in a ponytail, and the pale pink cover-up that just showed the top of her breasts. The Frisbee nearly hit his blonde head when he missed it. Ellie waved at him with two fingers and turned her gaze back to Rebecca.

"We should talk to them," Ellie said. "It could be fun."

Rebecca laughed. "They're not interested in me," she said. She'd barely even spoken to a boy before. Dad and Uncle Fredrick didn't count, nor did Tess's boyfriend, since he was obviously off limits.

Ellie waved her hand. "You're being silly."

Rebecca sighed and looked back at the boys, and then at the girls watching them on the lawn, with their flared skirts and bright red lips and delicate curls. Rebecca's wild, frizzy hair was nothing like theirs, not that Rebecca cared. She had never been particularly interested in boys.

A girl with beautiful ginger waves and a smattering of freckles on her pale cheeks glanced back with vividly green eyes. She wore a pale pink skirt that contrasted horribly with her hair, but she didn't seem to pay it any mind. Rebecca recognized her from the pool she sometimes went to with Ginny and Tess. Margot, Rebecca recalled. Margot seemed to recognize her too because she smiled and waved to Rebecca by the shore, and Rebecca grinned back.

"Oh, which one are you smiling at?" Ellie asked, peering around Rebecca.

Rebecca's face fell. "No one," she said, quickly looking away. It didn't matter if Ellie knew she was looking at Margot, or it shouldn't, but if she did, she might invite those girls over there. The thought made Rebecca's stomach do nervous backflips.

Ellie flopped down onto her back, her hair spread out behind her in a dark fan. "You're no fun," she said.

"You know," Rebecca said, "if I'd been a boy, you probably wouldn't have been able to go to school regardless. Mom and Dad would have sent a son to school."

"Probably," Ellie said. "They're old-fashioned that way."

Rebecca laughed, feeling only the tiniest bit of guilt settle in her gut. Of course she and Ellie knew what their parents had been through. In fifth grade, Rebecca learned about the Holocaust in school for the first time. When she came home the day of their first lesson, she taught Ellie what she knew, and they immediately went to their parents.

When Mom wouldn't answer their questions and Dad gave them stilted, half-formed descriptions of what life had been like before they left Germany, Rebecca and Ellie asked Uncle Fredrick. He told them about mom's brother Eli, the mysterious "other brother," and Eli's wife Susan, who had been Uncle Fredrick's parents. He told them about coming to America on an unsteady ship, the suffocating fear just as nauseating as the choppy water. He told them about saying goodbye to his brother and taking on a sister.

That night, Ellie tried to stifle her tears against her pillow, but Rebecca heard her crying until far too late. After Ellie went to bed, Rebecca imagined losing her sister the way Mom had lost Eli or Uncle Fredrick had lost his brother and she stuffed her face between her own pillows to stop herself from screaming.

"Mama!"

Presently, Ellie sat up and Rebecca stood. A young girl, one of the ones playing by the water, had somehow ended up in the river, struggling to stay upright. Ellie was suddenly on her feet, running. She dove into the water from the shore and swam, her arms moving in perfect circles even though she hadn't been in the water in years. Rebecca followed her to the edge and stopped, waiting.

Ellie scooped up the girl and began kicking. Slow, methodical. The young girl cried in Ellie's arms. Rebecca watched her sister struggle and the girl sob. She only screamed harder when Ellie stopped kicking.

"Ellie?" Rebecca called, but her sister didn't answer her. From this distance, Rebecca saw Ellie's mouth opening and closing, gasping. She couldn't breathe.

She told Uncle Fred I have a weak heart—

Rebecca's own heart pounded against her rib cage. She waded out into the water and dove, frantically paddling. What was the fastest way? Did she bend her knees or keep them straight? In the chaos of the moment, she couldn't remember how to swim properly. Her soaked skirt weighed heavily against her legs under the water.

She reached Ellie and the girl and took them both in her arms. Next to her, one of the boys from the Frisbee game took the little girl and gestured for Rebecca to swim. She hadn't heard him enter the water behind her.

Rebecca side stroked back to the edge of the water, straining her ears to hear Ellie gasping in her arms. But was she? Or was that the sound of Rebecca's own breath catching?

Two of the other boys (including the one who had gaped at Ellie earlier) pulled them both onto the shore. The blond boy flipped Ellie over and leaned over her face, pinching her nose and breathing hard into her mouth. The other boy thumped hard on her chest.

"El–Ellie." Rebecca sputtered, choking on water. Behind her, she heard the little girl sobbing. Her clothes clung to her skin and weighed her down, or that might have been preemptive grief that made her so heavy.

Someone must have called an ambulance somehow. They arrived in a whir of flashing lights and blaring sirens, or maybe they didn't, and then they were taking Ellie from her arms, only stopping when Rebecca screamed.

One of the men—a boy, really, not much older than Rebecca herself—knelt down in the grass beside her. "Sweetheart, we have to take your friend, all right?" Rebecca shook her head and the man said, "We have to make her better, ok? But we can't do that while you're holding onto her." Reluctantly, Rebecca let go, but she followed closely to Ellie on her stretcher.

The EMTs let Rebecca in the back for the ride to the hospital, even though she was still screaming and crying like that little girl in the water, or maybe because she was so distraught in the first place. She held Ellie's river-slicked hand the whole way to the hospital. Under her damp fingers she felt gently, then more firmly for Ellie's pulse, a soft beat against her skin to let Rebecca know that there was still hope. She never found it.

In the aftermath of her sister's death, Rebecca found solace in Margot, who approached her in the supermarket one day not long after the funeral and grabbed her arm. Margot's auburn hair hung in a loose braid over her freckled shoulder. She introduced herself as Tess's friend from the pool.

"I was there when your sister drowned," she said. "I'm so sorry."

"Thank you," Rebecca had said. "I really appreciate that." She liked the way Margot said "drowned" instead of "passed away" or "went on to a better place." No one wanted to acknowledge that Ellie was dead, but that didn't stop her from being so. If Rebecca had to hear one more person say "may her memory be a blessing," she was going to lose it.

"Anyway, if you and your family ever need anything ..." She trailed off and another girl their age called, "Margot! We're heading out."

"Well, bye," Margot said, and turned to follow her friends. Rebecca watched her leave. That night, the polka-dot pattern on Margot's dress weaved in and out of Rebecca's dreams. Margot's freckled face came closer and closer until their lips brushed and Rebecca woke, gasping from fear and elation all at once.

What would Ellie think of Rebecca's new friend? They had never spoken about homosexuality before, never entertained the thought that one of them could find another woman alluring the way Rebecca did Margot. Rebecca had never spoken about it at all, except briefly with Tess and Ginny and once with Uncle Fred. She hoped Ellie would understand. She couldn't imagine otherwise, that her kind and caring sister would have cast her out for such a thing. Rebecca wasn't sure how she herself felt about it, but she knew she shouldn't seek advice, especially not from her parents.

Rebecca ran into Margot again at the pool not long after that, sitting at the edge of the water with her feet in the deep end. Margot looked up, shielding her eyes against the sun, and beamed when she realized who it was casting shade over her freckled legs. "Hey," she said. "I was wondering when I'd see you."

"I'm waiting for my friends," Rebecca said, sitting beside Margot. "You're welcome to join us."

"I'd love to," Margot said. When Rebecca got home later that evening and Uncle Fredrick asked her what she was smiling about (her parents now seemed to frown upon smiling in any form), Rebecca said she'd spoken to a cute boy at the pool.

·

The year after Ellie drowned, Rebecca spent most of her time with Margot. They went to the pool when Rebecca wasn't waitressing and walked into downtown for milkshakes after, always strawberry, the same color as Margot's hair. When school began again and the pool closed, they walked side by side in Prospect Park and tried on the fanciest pillbox hats they could find at stores they couldn't afford. They talked about Rebecca's dreams to go to college, and Margot encouraged her to take community classes. "You're so smart, Bex."

"I'm not that smart." Ellie was smarter. Though now that Ellie was gone ...

But that was a horrible thought as well.

Rebecca confided in Margot about Ellie's death, how her parents had completely fallen apart, how she felt like the wrong child died. Margot never judged her, never said, "Oh c'mon now," or, worse, "You know they love you, Rebecca." She just let Rebecca speak. No one had ever done that for her before besides Ellie.

It was a warm night in August when Margot slipped her hand into Rebecca's as they walked along the ocean on Coney Island. They went to Coney Island often, in fact. Just the week before at one of the games, Margot had won a sheet of blue butterfly stickers for Rebecca that were far too pretty for her to ever use, but she treasured them all the same.

On the pier that night, with Margot's soft hand in hers, it was like nothing had changed, even though everything had. Margot led her under the boardwalk and stood close, her hands in Rebecca's, Rebecca's back against the wooden beam. Slowly, Margot reached up and cupped Rebecca's face in her hands, fingers caressing Rebecca's cheeks with such care Rebecca wanted to cry. Margot moved forward slowly, giving Rebecca plenty of time to back away. When she didn't, and when Margot's lips finally met hers, warm and soft as she had imagined, Rebecca kissed her back.

·

In the end, Rebecca didn't regret breaking it off between them. At least, that was what she told herself. Her wonderful, vibrant, beautiful Margot would have been shunned had they continued their forbidden romance. Her Margot, whom she wouldn't have been able to be with even if one of them had been a man. Margot wasn't Jewish.

"I don't understand," Margot said when Rebecca had explained everything. "I love you."

"You don't," Rebecca said. "You can't."

"Oh." Margot stood. They were at Margot's house, her parents away for the weekend. Margot's older brothers had both moved out years earlier.

"Margot–"

"Just leave." Margot had her back to Rebecca now, her shoulders shaking slightly. Rebecca turned and hesitated, just for a moment. If she stayed with Margot, Ginny and Tess would support them, or she thought so, and Uncle Fred would take them in. Of the latter, she was sure. When they could afford it, she and Margot would buy a house together and adopt a child, a boy, and … But it was no use. In no version of reality did Rebecca see her parents and Margot both existing in her life.

If she had to pick one, she would pick her family every time.

Rebecca turned around and left, biting hard on her lower lip to keep herself from crying. She tasted metal on her tongue where she used to taste Margot.

She heard from Tess later that Margot had gone to school upstate somewhere, that she was going to be a nurse, that she had a girlfriend she loved very much. After, Rebecca went home and sobbed into her pillow. She had done the right thing, Rebecca told herself. This had to be the right thing.

.

The following summer, nearly a year after Ellie's death, only one thing set Mom's eyes alight. One thing made her forget, just for a moment, that her younger and favorite daughter was dead. "You need to find yourself a man," she said over and over.

Rebecca would sigh, resist the urge to roll her eyes, and say, "I know, Mom."

"I have many friends with sons," she said.

"I know, Mom."

But Rebecca didn't need Mom's help to find herself a husband. It was Ginny who introduced her to Silas one afternoon by the pool. Silas was Ginny's cousin and a lifeguard, older. He had already finished college and would start a job in September. Rebecca was working as a waitress and taking classes at the community college.

"He's cute," Tess said after Silas had left them. He'd shaken Tess's and Rebecca's hands, his fingers lingering perhaps longer than they should have on the back of Rebecca's wrist. She couldn't yet decide if the chills that had broken out down her arm were good or bad.

"He's my cousin," Ginny said, swatting Tess's shoulder. "And you have a boyfriend."

Tess shrugged. "I still have eyes," she said.

Rebecca glanced back at Silas, who was looking over at her. His blue eyes hid under his sunglasses. His hair was a pale brown, his cheeks freckle-less. He came over to Rebecca later, after his shift, and asked her to get a shake with him at the diner sometime this week. She heard herself say yes as if from a great distance. Her friends giggled about it for the rest of the day.

.

"Ginny talks about you all the time," Rebecca said. She didn't know where that had come from. Before he started life-guarding, Ginny had never mentioned Silas except to talk about the annoying cousins she had to see over the holidays.

He shrugged. "You're just saying that," he said, but he grinned all the same.

The waiter came over with their shake. Silas had consented to share if they could get vanilla, so Rebecca compromised by putting strawberries on top. She watched him sip their dessert through a straw and wondered how Ellie would handle this. Ellie had had a much better handle on boys than Rebecca did. More than once, Rebecca wondered if something was wrong with her, especially after Margot. Her mother's voice in her head, but she realized that too late.

.

Vietnam loomed over their heads. It loomed over everyone, but Silas seemed especially fearful of the draft. "I don't know what my parents will do without me," he said. "They need me."

"Maybe the war will end soon," Rebecca said. "And then you could stay here." *With me*, she thought, but she couldn't quite bring herself to say it. They'd been dating for several months now, but too often Rebecca felt like an actress, like she was playing the role of Silas Rogers' girlfriend instead of really being Silas Rogers' girlfriend. It hadn't been this way with Margot.

The two of them stretched out on Silas's bed in his childhood room, both of them fully clothed. Silas had his arm around Rebecca, and she fought the urge to squirm away.

"It won't," Silas said. "My buddy John was just drafted. He tried to get his girlfriend to marry him, before, but she was going to school."

Rebecca sat up. "What do you mean?"

"Oh, you know, they're saying now that if you're married, you can't be deployed—"

"So let's get married." The words left Rebecca's mouth of their own volition, springing into the air from her lips like they were their own living beings, but she knew they were right.

Silas frowned at her, his eyebrows contracted. "I don't want to make you," he said, even though he had brought it up in the first place. Rebecca was sure he meant to introduce the idea, even if slowly.

"You wouldn't be," Rebecca said. "I want to. I love you." It wasn't the first time Rebecca had said that to Silas, but it was the first time she hadn't stumbled over the words, the first time they hadn't tasted rancid on her tongue, even if she wasn't sure that she meant it. She could not lose Silas, not like this. Not when she could save him like she couldn't save Ellie. Even if she had to lie to do it.

Silas's face split into a grin. "I love you too," he said, and he kissed her.

—

Rebecca was fourteen when Uncle Fred met Nina. She was from Germany too, a refugee from the war that had claimed the rest of her family. Once or twice, Rebecca overheard them speaking German together. She'd never heard her uncle speak the language before. Even when Mom or Dad would speak German to Uncle Fred, he always spoke English back.

Mom was elated, and she often made it her business to say so. "It is about time you settle down," she told him.

Uncle Fred glanced at Rebecca, who shot him a small smile. He folded his arms where he sat on the living room couch and said, "I don't know about settle. I just met her."

"You like her, no?" Uncle Fred nodded and Mom said, "You are going to be an old man before you marry." She weaved a needle and thread through an old shirt of Ellie's that Ellie had ripped playing on the playground the day before.

"I'm thirty-three, Gabi."

"Humph. I was starting to think you might be a queer." She said it with a little laugh at the end of the sentence, like she'd just told the funniest joke in the world. Rebecca didn't see what was so hilarious about being gay. Though Rebecca hadn't yet met Margot, Tess had already confided in Rebecca a few months prior that her uncle was gay. Tess's uncle was one of the nicest people Rebecca knew.

Uncle Fred frowned. "There wouldn't be anything wrong with that," he said.

"It is illegal for a reason. It is not natural, you know."

"That's ignorant, Gabi."

Mom didn't respond, and Uncle Fred switched to German to say something too quickly for Rebecca to understand.

Mom nearly dropped Ellie's shirt. "Don't you dare put us in the same boat as them."

"'Us' and 'them' is exactly the problem," Uncle Fredrick said. "Excuse me." He got up and slipped out the door. Rebecca heard his footsteps down the hall and Ellie's voice, curious. Uncle Fred mumbled something in response and then Rebecca heard the front door open.

Several days after that, Rebecca asked Uncle Fred what he had said to Mom. She worried he wouldn't remember, but Uncle Fred told her with only a brief hesitation. "They rounded up the homosexuals just like they did us," he said. "We were illegal too. No human being should ever have to go through what we went through, Rebecca."

But before that, in the living room with her mother and an awkward silence, Mom resumed her sewing.

"Ignore him," she said without looking directly at Rebecca. "He does not know what he is talking about." She set the needle aside. "You know, Leviticus states that for man to lie with man as he lies with a woman is an abomination." Rebecca hadn't known, but she nodded anyway.

Years later, when Rebecca's cousin Zane brought his boyfriend Henry home to meet the family, Rebecca asked Mom, who had just turned eighty, what she thought. Mom shrugged and said, "It is strange. But family is everything, Rebecca. I will not turn him away." Rebecca didn't know whether to laugh or cry.

—

"I wish I had my dress here," Mom said to Rebecca the day of Rebecca's wedding to Silas. She ran her fingers over Rebecca's hair, done up in a bun atop her head. Two perfect curls hung on either side of Rebecca's face, though Rebecca supposed her veil would obscure all their hard work.

"It's ok, Mom," she said. "We could afford a new one." She currently wore only a thin black robe, patterned with roses across the hem.

"That is not why," Mom said, and she sat across from Rebecca. They were sitting in a classroom at the temple before the wedding. Any moment now, Ginny and Tess would come with the veil and the dress. Ginny would be her bridesmaid, since Rebecca would be Tess's when Tess married in three months' time and Tess would be Ginny's one day. Ginny had an older brother, but neither she nor Tess had sisters. Perhaps Rebecca didn't either. She wasn't sure, now that Ellie had died, if either of them could be referred to as such.

"Why, then?" Rebecca asked.

Mom offered her the ghost of a smile. Once, when she was younger, Rebecca had called her "Mama," and Mom shook her head. "Say it the American way," she had said. "Say 'Mom.'"

Now, sitting across from Rebecca in a Hebrew school class-room, she said, "Because my mama wore that dress. And her mama." She took Rebecca's hand and said, "It just—I would have liked to see it on one of my daughters."

"Yeah," Rebecca said. *One of my daughters.* Rebecca pulled her hand away and stood. Mom was one of those people who acted like Ellie was still out there, somewhere, if only they could find her.

As she joined Silas at the altar, stomach in knots and head swimming, she thought of Margot. A part of her she swore was wrong wanted it to be Margot up there with her. Margot she was marrying, if she had to marry so young. Rebecca even smelled like Margot that day, the peppermint perfume she had always worn, because Rebecca had gotten some to remind herself.

Her parents loved Silas. Just a week before the wedding, Silas had come over for dinner. He complimented the meal and Mom was gone, fawning over him like he was the best thing to ever happen to their family. "I always wanted a son," she said. Dad asked Silas all about his family, his history, his future plans while Silas basked in the attention. Rebecca kept quiet. The last time she'd spoken out of turn in front of Silas, she'd gotten a fist-sized bruise over a set of searing ribs for her trouble.

Silas smiled at her the whole wedding service and kissed her when they were meant to kiss and stomped on the glass under his shoe. Later, when he took her into bed, Rebecca told herself she enjoyed it, or if she didn't, that the first time was always like this (the first time with Margot didn't count, of course). It would get better. And when married men were no longer exempt from the draft, only fathers, she told herself that she wanted to get pregnant. She still wanted to save him.

Chapter Six: Lately
2001-2022

You hadn't actually seen the infamous video circulating the Twitterverse (yet another one) until your best friend, Dana, texted asking for your opinion. *Miranda!!! R u following the Lauren Wolf fiasco?* You hadn't even known there was a fiasco to follow, but it seems like someone is always texting you about the news lately.

A quick Google search pulled up the video in which actress and talk show host Lauren Wolf made bold and inflammatory claims about the Holocaust in front of millions of viewers on live TV. The Holocaust wasn't about race, she said, but rather how awful man can be to their fellow man. Your stomach tightened, but you read the subsequent article anyway. You read how Lauren had been suspended for the next two weeks and her network's assurance that they stood with the Jewish community. You texted Dana back an affirmative. *Yeah, it's wild.*

But even now that you saw it, you were torn. No, Judaism wasn't a race, but the Nazis thought it was, and an inferior race at that. The thing that scared you most, though, was Lauren's apology. While she said she regretted her actions and promised to do better in the future (politicians, take note), how had

Lauren Wolf not known, as she claimed, that the Nazis saw Jews as subhuman? The whole thing was an indictment of the US education system, truly. In your time living in Indianapolis, you'd met more than one person for whom you were their first Jewish acquaintance. At least one had been shocked you hadn't had horns.

You brought it up to your partner, Bree, when Bree came home from work that day, shrugging their pleather jacket from their broad shoulders and passing you a bag of takeout. You'd watched this morning as they twisted their dark hair up in a half-bun, half-braid, a hairstyle you have to admit looked remarkably good on them, even knowing they'd done it in a rush. These last few weeks, Bree frequently had to finish their morning routine halfway out the door, slipping on a shoe as they ran down the stairs or finishing a protein bar as they rushed to their car. Bree hadn't yet readjusted to nine-to-five office life after working from home for nearly two years. You were still working from home, evidenced by your freshly showered hair and checkered pajama pants. All your clothes seemed perpetually dotted with ginger fur from the cat using your laundry pile as a pillow before you put your clothes away.

"Have you seen what's happening with Lauren Wolf?" you asked.

Bree sighed an affirmative. "Of course I have," they said, as though you'd both been playing close attention to the fallout for the last three days. They probably believed you had been, at any rate.

You sat together at the marble island you occasionally used to cook and more often used to collect magazines you got in the mail, almost always addressed to an old occupant even though you and Bree had lived in your apartment for four years. You and Bree met over a decade ago at a protest with Jewish Voice for Peace. Bree wasn't Jewish or Palestinian, but they had been there as part of a Black-Palestinian solidarity contingent.

"I hope they're not going to fire her," Bree said between bites of dumpling. Your partner kept up with all things anti-Semitism, everything happening in Israel and Palestine. Their knowledge often made you feel less Jewish, inadequate in some way. You tried not to mention it, even if Bree was perfectly understanding when you did. It wasn't anyone else's fault but your own.

"They're not," you say. "Two weeks suspension." Part of you was proud you can deliver that news, at least.

"A white woman would have gotten a slap on the wrist."

"Probably," you said. "Remember when Linda Swift did that whole Hitler sketch and had a movie announced like a year later?" Old photos from that sketch had been circulating through social media for the last day or so. Now you knew why.

Bree reached over and helped themselves to fried rice. "The next person to tell me anti-Semitism doesn't exist," they said, "is going to get slapped."

———

You didn't think about religion often. You hadn't gone to temple since your niece's consecration and you likely wouldn't be back until your nephew's. Before that, aside from the occasional wedding or funeral, the last time you'd been was for you and your brother's Hebrew school graduation nearly fourteen years prior, much longer ago than you liked to think about. When had you both gotten so old?

These days, you were more likely to think of Christian fundamentalism when you thought of religion at all, unless there were Jews on the news. The Lauren Wolf video. Anti-Semitism on the rise in the early days of the COVID pandemic. Or on the other side, the Israeli government bombing the shit out of Gaza just a few months ago. That, too, had set off a wave of anti-Semitism that left you nervous for your father and brother, both of whom still attended temple regularly (the former) and semi-regularly (the latter). You still hadn't decided if those nerves were selfish in the face of what the Palestinians in Gaza had gone through, still went through. You talked about it some with your therapist.

Naturally, you attending anti-occupation protests and reposting resources for Palestinian followers on Instagram led to accusations of anti-Semitism against you and plenty of family arguments. Your aunt, your late mother's twin, won't speak with you anymore and your cousins sent you endless articles about why the generations-long Israeli occupation of Palestine and the genocide of its residents by the Israeli government were perfectly justified.

Though you would be hard pressed to remember the last time you prayed, you had never really believed in a god. Still, you had prayed because it meant something to your dad, especially the Kaddish. He said it every week while you were growing up, for your mom and for his own, so you had said it as well. On the days your family couldn't attend temple for whatever reason, he did it on his own, sending a quick prayer out to whoever was listening that the women he'd loved and lost were safe.

When they learned you recited the Kaddish during nightly services, your summer camp friends interrogated you endlessly. "If you don't believe in a god, why do you say the prayers?" they asked. Or else, they simply shot you strange looks during services.

You shrugged or wrote it off as a habit, but never told them the real reason. You had always been close to your dad, especially after your mom died. It wasn't until you were older that you realized how much he sacrificed to be there for you and Noah, the jobs he turned down so he could be there for you after school and on the weekends, even though it meant money had been uncomfortably tight in the years after your mother's death. Even as a child, though, you felt his love and gave love freely in return.

Still, to acknowledge such a thing wasn't exactly cool as a teen and besides, you didn't want to be the girl with the dead mom. Jamie Cohen's parents were only divorced and she talked about it constantly. You knew every detail of her dad's affair, of the court case, of her step family's convoluted dynamic (everyone knew about Jamie's new step-brother's half-brother and their rivalry), and you heard how the other girls talked about her. "She's so self-centered." "Just shut up." No, thank you.

Your biggest fear as a child—besides being the Jamie Cohen of dead moms—was that your friends would find out you went to therapy. You only told Dana, whose dad died the year before you met and whose mother also took her to a therapist against her will. You couldn't remember much of your mom, since you were only three when a gunman murdered her and half a dozen others in a brutal act of gun violence, but Dad put you in therapy anyway. As an adult, you understood. Of course he put his kids in therapy after they lost their mom. As a kid, though, you were only embarrassed and resentful. What if the other kids found out you were a freak who needed a shrink?

You didn't think about your mom back then, or you tried not to. Besides, you loved Henry, your dad's partner and basically your stepfather at that point, and how could you miss a person you barely remembered? Henry Chen had been there for most of your life, since you and Noah were six years old. He was a second dad in every way but legally.

So what if seeing the other girl scouts at the mother-daughter picnic rankled? Get over it, you told yourself. No need to be so dramatic. Up until you were ten or so, you told your friends you and Noah were adopted and you never had a mom. It helped that you both looked more like her than your dad, with narrow noses and slightly-crowded smiles. Your dark hair was still lighter than your dad's, whose hair was almost black. You got away with it until one of the other parents, looking to adopt, asked Dad about the process.

You never thought about the steady rise in gun violence your whole life in the context of your own mother's death either, not until you were eleven or so. You were in final period Spanish when your teacher announced there would be a shooting drill the following day, which basically involved the students pressing themselves up against the wall for five minutes before the principal came over the loudspeaker and ended the drill. They'd gone over the drill with you before, at an assembly early on in the year, although you had never done one.

You hated Spanish, so that was fine with you. Unlike Dad, who was fluent in English, German, and French, you never learned another language and struggled with simple conjugations and pronouns. The worst part was that Noah had the foresight to take French so Dad could help him study for his tests. You told him that was cheating every time you caught them working at the kitchen table through unintelligible vocab words. Noah shrugged and said, "Not really. I'm still learning it." That always infuriated you more, how level-headed your twin was.

All of which was to say, you weren't upset in the slightest about the prospect of starting Spanish a few minutes late. The afternoon of the drill, the principal came over the loudspeaker and announced that the students were to huddle up against the walls, lights off, and make not a sound for the next five minutes or so. You huddled against the wall with your classmates, the only sounds heavy breathing, the occasional nervous giggle, and a shout from one of the boys trying to irk the teacher, who only sighed and shook her head.

Two minutes in, your leg was numb from crouching beside the wall and you sort of had to pee when the dark shape of a man appeared in the doorway. The girl beside you gasped and your whole body went rigid. The air grew colder, even though nothing had changed. The man reached forward and the door-knob shook. One of your classmates muffled a scream behind you. The man walked away. Someone near you let out a heavy exhale. The air in the room returned to its normal temperature and you tried not to cry. Not minutes later, someone came back over the loudspeaker and said that you'd all passed the drill and to, "Please resume your lessons."

The rest of the period, you did your best to focus on the tangle of verbs on the white board at the front of the room, but your mind was a jumble of images and sounds. The teacher in the hallway, whoever he was, highlighted by the florescent light. The half-scream of one of your classmates. Had your mom screamed like that when she saw the gunman enter the temple? Had she seen the gunman, or had he blown off her head before she'd realized what was happening? You tightened your grip on your pencil and watched the clock for the duration of the lesson.

About two minutes before the end of the day, another voice came over the loudspeaker. "Miranda Altenberg to the nurse's office. Miranda Altenberg to the nurse's office." You looked up at your teacher, who nodded for you to go amid a collective "Ohhh" from your classmates. It wasn't like you were going to the principal's office, for crying out loud. You never got in trouble at school.

The hallway was still dark, several classrooms seemingly empty. You walked quicker past those doors. In your head, the shadow-man couldn't be a teacher but some unknown *he* ready to jump out at you with a gun, and those cavernous classrooms were a perfect hiding place.

You took the corners slowly, too, just in case. *He* could be waiting there, ready to jump, ready to fire. Every shadow was a shooter, every little noise the crack of a gunshot. At one point, someone down the hall laughed and you raised your hands to your mouth to cover a scream. By the time you got to the nurse's office, your hands were shaking and you had to steady your breathing.

You didn't know what to expect in the nurse's office, but it certainly wasn't Noah, huddled on a cot, face red from sobbing, with a pensive Henry beside him. Henry had an arm slung over Noah's shoulder and appeared near tears himself. You looked back and forth between them. "What happened?" you asked Noah, once more struggling to hold back a sob of your own. You rarely cried, then or now, but seeing Noah in tears had always been a surefire way to get you going.

The bell rang and you heard the thunder of freed students up and down the halls.

"He had a hard time with the shooting drill," Henry said, his voice strained. "I'm taking you home."

Usually, they took the bus. This was years before Henry began using a wheelchair full-time, but he already dealt with chronic pain and often had a hard time driving. Dad worked until four most days, ever since you'd gone to middle school.

At home, you sat downstairs, pretending to work on your homework while straining to hear the muffled conversation between Noah and Henry in Dad and Henry's room. You couldn't make out the words, but you could make out the strained sobs from Noah and something like reassurance from Henry. At last, Dad burst through the door and raced into the living room. He wasn't crying outright, but his cheeks were bright and his eyes shining. It hit you then how whatever happened to your mom, Dad would have seen the shooter. Dad would have had plenty of time to scream.

You burst into tears, and Dad gathered you in his arms.

"It's ok," he said. "You're safe, baby. Did you do the drill too?" You nodded against his chest and Dad stroked your hair gently. "It's all right," he said. "It's ok. It wasn't real. You're safe." He said it to you as much as to himself.

.

You managed to keep the incident from your friends. The following day, you and Noah were both back at school from period one. Your dad drove you, even though it made him late for work, his hands vice-like on the steering wheel and his lips pressed into a thin white line. Henry rode along, his hand on Dad's arm, attempting to keep conversation light. You didn't have final period Spanish with any of your friends and no one seemed to remember that they'd called your name over the loudspeaker, though you had a lie prepared just in case, that you had to go home early for a funeral, a distant relative you had little connection to.

You spotted your brother laughing and joking with his friends at lunch like he hadn't just spent the night hysterical in your father's arms. After that, the school emailed all parents of any active shooter drills in advance. You and Noah often skipped them.

That summer, your second at camp, you confided in Dana, but until you were an adult, no one else knew what that drill had done to your family. No one else had to live with the memory of Noah's tear-stained face or Dad's hitched breaths in your ear as he did his best not to fall apart when you needed him.

You had the same, small, nerdy group of friends all five summers you were a camper. Noah, on the other hand, seemed friends with everyone and at least two of your own so-called BFFs had a crush on your twin at some point, the traitors. Still, it was hard to be mad at Noah for long, even when he would show up to camp dances every year with a different girl on his arm and you, openly bi from the age of fourteen on, went unnoticed by anyone of any gender.

You came out to your family first, perhaps a month before your third summer. You sat them down at dinner and said, "I think I like girls too."

Henry dropped his fork in a dramatic display of faux-rage. "What? How could you ever think we'd be ok with this?" Dad rolled his eyes. Noah laughed.

Dad addressed you directly. "Coming out isn't easy," he said. "Thank you for trusting us."

"Yeah, yeah," Noah said. "Guess we'll be competing for the same girls this summer, but I'll go easy on you."

"Noah," Dad warned lightly, but you were laughing. Despite your open family dynamics, you'd thought about coming out for weeks before you actually did it. To do so was freeing, a relief.

The camp you attended was one of many to send campers to Israel the summer after they turned sixteen. You overheard a whispered conversation one night between your dad and Henry a few months before you and Noah were to go on the trip, your first without your dad. Your first out of the country, period.

They stood just outside your room. "It's a lot of money," Dad said.

"We can afford it," Henry reassured him.

You kept quiet, suppressed the guilt attempting to unsettle your stomach. You wanted to go with your friends so badly and besides, your basically-a-second-dad had enough money to send you and Noah even without the scholarships you got, especially after Henry and his sister sold their mom's old house a few years ago. If only Dad weren't so damn proud.

"I don't want to ask you to do that."

"You're not," Henry said. "It's *our* money, Zane." Dad said something unintelligible after that. They slipped into their room and you couldn't hear them anymore.

The next morning, you pretended you hadn't heard anything at all. When Dad asked if you were all right in the morning, noting the bags under your eyes, you rolled your eyes and headed off to school.

You did go on the trip, which began with three days in the Czech Republic, specifically Prague, during which you took countless photos of your less camera-shy friends with your disposable camera. You marveled at the old brick architecture that lined the cobblestone streets and relished the taste of the sweet treats you bought in the village. The counselors took you on a tour of the city and led you through an old Jewish cemetery, but your friends were far more interested in the gift shops than in the history of long-dead men you didn't know and would never meet.

After that, you spent three days in Poland, a country which you were positive, in different circumstances, would have been delightful. For you, your memories of the place would consist almost entirely of old ghettos, concentration camps, and constant rain.

Setting foot in Auschwitz was surreal at best, nightmarish at worst, unhelped by the steady downpour that stuck your jacket to your skin and chilled you to the bone. Auschwitz, a place you'd heard about all your life, but so far away from your own reality, across time and space, and now here you were somehow, your Timberland-clad feet on the same ground your grandfather had fled Europe to escape. Your mother's parents had been imprisoned in another camp, one in Germany, but you couldn't help but think of them when you entered through the tall metal gate and read the inscription above. Arbeit macht frei. Work sets you free.

Your grandfather rarely spoke of the war. You supposed you might not either, had you lived through it. You knew some about his childhood, his family before he left home with your great-aunt and great-uncle, fleeing for their lives and, in a way, your own. You could make out the fuzzy history around your grandfather's story until he was twelve or so, and then time skipped until he met your grandmother, until he had his son.

Once, Noah asked him, "Did you want more kids, Grandpa?"

You must have been seven or eight at the time. "I didn't know I wanted any children," Grandpa said. "I did not know I would be able to keep them safe." It wasn't until many years later that you realized, having never been under threat of imprisonment for who you were, what he meant.

At Auschwitz, the scene of nightmarish unreality came and went and you weren't sure whether you preferred it or not to the conflicting sensation of being all too present. The worst part wasn't the dilapidated wooden barracks or even the rusted gas chambers perhaps the size of a small living room. No, the worst part was the museum, where a case of forcibly shaven human hair sat on display beside a mountain of faded baby shoes. Even your chatterbox brother was respectfully silent the whole trip. Tears ran down Dana's face the whole time and the two of you walked with hands linked.

The mood picked up when you flew into Tel Aviv with a brief layover in Berlin. Despite the armed soldiers traveling with you and the constant talk of bomb threats, none of you would appreciate what it meant until much later. Your friend, Penny, asked a counselor once, after hearing three IDF soldiers discuss the so-called conflict with Palestine for an hour (and placing the blame squarely on everyone but their own government), if they would hear at all from any Palestinians.

You hadn't considered this until Penny voiced her thought, but she wasn't wrong. You hadn't heard from a single Palestinian, nor was such a talk on the itinerary. The counselor looked at Penny like she'd just suggested they drive the bus off a mountain. No one brought it up again.

Two, nearly three weeks into the trip, six Israeli teens joined your cohort for five days. It was the moment you'd all been waiting for, ever since the counselors announced the impending exchange. The boys in your group had readied themselves for weeks to leer at the Israeli girls and the girls to lust after the Israeli boys. To everyone's surprise, the three new girls, all pretty enough to be models in your opinion, made easy conversation with your own friends. Shira, wavy golden-brown hair loose around her shoulders, clicked immediately with Penny, chattering away about anime and comic books and their long list of nerdy interests. Yael, shorter and curvier with stunning green eyes, sat toward the back of the group, talking with Dana and the others about American music. By the time you got back to the hotel, you felt like the three of them, Shira, Yael, and Roni, had been there the whole time.

You connected with Roni especially, a tall girl with wild, light brown hair and a quick wit. Her parents were Americans who'd made Aliyah before she was born. "But I've never been to the States," she said. "I'd love to." You were eating dinner together at your hotel for the week, interrogating the Israeli girls about their lives. Roni turned to you and grinned. "It'd be an excuse to visit you."

You nearly choked on your water. "What?"

"If I came to visit the States," Roni said.

"Oh," you said. "Yeah, I'd like that." Roni smiled and butterflies stirred in your stomach.

Your friends sat in the hotel lobby until late. Eleven o'clock came and went, then midnight, then one. It was nearly two o'clock in the morning when Shira and Dana said goodnight and you realized you and Roni were alone.

"It's late," you said, as though Roni wouldn't have picked up on this fact. Still, neither of you made a move to leave.

You stayed for another hour, talking about where you were from (Roni was born in Tel Aviv but lived in Haifa), the war (Roni wasn't sure exactly what she'd do once she was drafted into the IDF, much less about the occupation itself, but she did know she was hopeless at combat), and your families (Roni had three older sisters, two of whom had left for the army already and the last of whom was about to).

The conversation turned to what you liked to do for fun. You mentioned one of your favorite shows was *How I Met Your*

Mother and Roni reminded you that earlier in the evening, Dana had teased you about your massive crush on Cobie Smulders, who played Robin Scherbatsky on the show.

"Do you like women?" Roni asked.

"Yes," you said, your defenses suddenly up. You had never been closeted (your dad being in a years-long relationship with a man probably had something to do with that), but you also didn't know how this girl stood, even if you'd been flirting for the last few hours non-stop. Straight girls flirted with their friends all the time, so you never could tell, and spending the next four days (three now, technically) with a homophobe sounded like a terrible time for everyone involved.

"Me too," Roni said with a grin.

Oh? Oh! "Really?"

"Have you ever kissed someone before?" Roni asked. You shook your head and Roni asked, "Would you like to?"

You nodded slowly, unbelieving. No one had ever wanted to kiss you before. "Please," you said softly, and you did.

Years later, when you were with Bree and taking a trip to San Francisco, you met up with Roni, who was living there with her girlfriend. You, Bree, Roni, and Roni's girlfriend, Allie, met up outside a small cafe on the sunny side of a sloped street. It had been ten years since you had last seen Roni and if you didn't know any better, you would have said Roni was thriving. Her hair was wilder than ever, framing her head in a feathery halo. It was sixty degrees even, but Roni's skin remained deeply tanned. The freckles splashed across her nose and cheeks drew attention to her amber eyes. She looked good. She looked healthy.

"It's all a lie," Roni said with a dismissive wave of her hand when you complimented her on her appearance. "I'm a disaster."

After the IDF, Roni had moved to the Sates like she'd always planned. It took her six months to have a complete and total breakdown and another three before she was diagnosed with PTSD, depression, and anxiety from her time in the army. She still struggled with flashbacks, night terrors, panic attacks. She felt endless guilt about her parents' Aliyah, thinking about who their property used to belong to and what happened to them so two white American Jews could live on their land, even though she hadn't been born when her parents moved. Sometimes the anxiety would render her unable to eat and she would shed a dozen pounds in mere weeks.

"I've been working with Breaking the Silence," she said. "Have you heard of them?" Bree nodded and you shook your head. "Allie hadn't heard of them either," Roni said to you. "They're a group of ex-IDF soldiers who talk about the fucked-up things they're made to do in the army." Roni didn't say what those things might be. You were afraid to ask, though you could infer.

"Anyway," Roni said, stirring her tea with the end of a plastic fork. "How have you been?"

—

Dana was the only person you still spoke to regularly from that time in your life. You called her the morning after viewing the Lauren video. She was still working from home too.

"I'm just tired," Dana said in response. "Like, how is this still a conversation we're having?" Dana was still a part of her local synagogue and much more deeply involved in her Jewish community than you ever were. She and her fiancé, who was Palestinian, made frequent trips to Gaza to protest the occupation. At least, they had before the pandemic. Since March 2020, no one you knew had traveled much. Certainly not out of the country.

Your cat, an orange fuzzball called Wanda after Marvel's Scarlet Witch, leaped onto your lap. You traced patterns in her fur with one finger. "Yeah," you said. It wasn't Dana's fault, but you always felt like you weren't entitled to an opinion on Jewish current events when you spoke to your old friend, much the same way you felt with Bree. Dana was more informed, more invested. At camp, Dana used to tease you that you were Jew-ish since you didn't even believe in a god. She'd since apologized for that, but you couldn't help the small voice in the back of your mind that said Dana had been right all those years ago.

"Anyway," Dana said, "how's your family?" Dana had been one of your traitor friends to crush on Noah during their time at camp, which you'd laughed about together in the nearly two decades since.

"Good," you said. "I saw them a few months ago for my niece's consecration." Neither you (who'd stayed in Indianapolis after college) nor Noah (now living in Washington Heights) sought out a temple of any kind until Noah met his current wife, who had her own. It saved them from shopping around for the wedding after Noah proposed, the same way they would shop around for a florist or a photographer. Noah and Amy attended largely for the occasional High Holy Day service until Hallie, Noah's firstborn, turned five and they enrolled her in temporarily-virtual Hebrew school.

"I wasn't sure if he would," Dad admitted to you one day before Hallie's consecration. It was about a year and a half after the start of the pandemic. You had come to stay with Dad and Henry after extensive quarantining and COVID testing, both at your own prerogative. Your Crohn's treatment and Henry's MS meds left you both immunocompromised, but when you offered to find a hotel because of it, Henry pushed you to stay with them anyway. He never told you outright, but you had always been close and you knew how much it hurt him that you stayed away for him, to protect him. You came, but you insisted on waiting at least two weeks after seeing friends at a local diner and isolating yourself in your old room for a day before you could get rapid test results post-flight.

"Would what?" you asked. You, Dad, and Henry were sitting around the coffee table in the living room playing Scrabble, a game Dad always seemed to win. You hadn't seen either of them in over a year because of the pandemic. Dad had gone almost entirely gray in the meantime, the lines on his face deeper than the last time you'd gotten together in person. Henry was the same, eyes sharp behind thick glasses and smile bright. The newest thing about Henry was an updated wheelchair, which he'd wasted no time showing off to you.

"Enroll the kids," Dad said. "It didn't seem like either of you cared so much." It was a casual sentence, but the hurt dripped from his words. He wasn't wrong, either. Noah had said before that he only joined a temple because it meant a lot to his wife, and you hadn't sought out a Jewish community at all. Henry's eyes flickered up from his letters, but neither of you said anything in response.

Dad looked up from the board. "You don't need to feel bad," he said.

"I don't feel bad," you said. A lie. You both knew it.

"I'm trying to think," Henry muttered, returning to his letters. It had been his turn for five minutes now. Henry notoriously took the most time to use his letters. He also refused to play with a timer.

"He's going to win anyway," you said of your dad. "We're playing for second."

"Sure, but you came in second the last time we played," Henry muttered to himself. He leaned forward to play "wrong" off of your "over," just missing the triple word score. Naturally, Dad had an S.

The consecration itself took place at Noah's temple a few days into your trip. The cantor led Hallie's small class of masked four- and five-year-olds in the Sh'ma and the rabbi gifted them all with miniature Torahs they could scarcely read in English, much less Hebrew. You gave your niece a quick hug and she grinned at you. She had just lost two of her front teeth, but you wouldn't know that if you hadn't seen unmasked photos on Facebook just a few days ago. Today, she wore a KN95 in pale pink, her favorite color, over the freckles that splashed across her pointed nose. Noah or his wife had tied her curly auburn hair into a loose ponytail. She looked like her mom in a lot of ways—they had the same red hair and Hallie was already one of the tallest in her class—but her eyes were all Noah's. They were yours, and your mom's.

"Did you see my project?" Hallie asked. You told her you hadn't, and she showed you the wall where the Hebrew school educator had posted twenty short, handwritten assignments by the students. A cluster of chattering five-year-olds quickly distracted Hallie and she ran off, but you found her assignment and read, *My name is Hallie Jaqueline Altenberg. I'm named after my grandmother. Her name was Helena Altenberg. My dad is also named after his grandma. His name is Noah and her name was Nina. My Hebrew name is Eleora and it means God is light. I love my name because it is pretty and because it makes me feel close to my grandma even though I never met her.*

Noah came up beside you as you finished. "Congrats," you said. His pale pink mask matched Hallie's.

"Thanks," he laughed. "I don't know that I did anything. The cantor taught them the songs and Hallie wrote the little name assignment."

"She had help."

"I won't tell if you don't," he said.

You looked over at Hallie, who was showing off her new Torah to her mom. "Did we get mini Torahs when we did this?" you asked Noah.

"Oh yeah, we decorated the covers too," Noah said. "I think I still have mine."

"You don't," Dad said, coming up behind you. "I have them both. They're in the basement."

Noah laughed again. "Oops. I keep saying I'll come clear out my old stuff and I never do."

"I don't mind," Dad said, a hand on Noah's shoulder. "It's an excuse for you to come back."

—

If you really thought about it, you might have separated your activism life into pre- and post-Israel. Post-Israel started three days after you and Noah returned to the States, the night you had dinner with your maternal grandparents, who'd come to New York to catch up with their grandbabies and hear about their trip.

"Did you love it?" your grandmother asked over the candlelit table at the in-hotel restaurant. As a kid, you loved your grandparents' Hungarian accents, even though you never heard your grandparents speak Hungarian. Both wore long sleeves, even though it was still August. They hated the faded, blue numbers that tattooed their forearms. You didn't blame them.

It was just you, Noah, and your grandparents, though you would have preferred Dad there as a buffer. You never quite knew what to say to the couple who had left your family to struggle alone after your mother's death. At this point in your life, you didn't know all the details, but you knew Dad had fallen into a deep depression after your mother died, that you were scraping by at best until Henry. You'd never *felt* poor, but then again, all of this happened before second grade.

Dad tried his best to hide his depression from you too, so you didn't realize how bad it was until you were older. He still had the (albeit rarer) occasional morning he couldn't get out of bed or a night he had to shut himself up in the room he shared with Henry. The one time you went to check on him at age nine or ten, you'd done so with purpose, slipping away while Henry was making dinner to see where Dad had gone off to.

Dad had gotten home that night after work, whispered something to Henry, and went to go lie in their room. The lights were all off, so you'd turned them on by instinct. Dad, who'd been lying under a tall pile of blankets, blinked quickly and wiped the tears from his cheeks. He tacked on a too-wide smile for your benefit and he looked so unlike himself that you didn't know whether to run or cry. Henry came not a minute later and ushered you away. In the kitchen, Henry sat you at the table and pulled up a chair for himself.

"Do you want to talk about what just happened?" You shook your head and Henry said, "Do you think we should, though?"

You shrugged. "I don't know." You'd never seen your dad like that before. You wondered if he was really sick or if he would die like Mom.

Henry shifted in his seat. "Sometimes," he said, "your dad gets really sad. It isn't anything you or me or Noah did. He just gets that way."

You studied your hands. "Ok," you said, even though you had so much else to say. You got sad sometimes, but not like that. There had to be a reason for such sadness, right? Wasn't there any way to make it better?

You didn't want to think about the scary, strange smile you'd seen on your dad's face in the bedroom, so you didn't mention any of that. Henry let you go, but you had a hard time sleeping that night. Dad was fine the next day, or so he claimed, but you couldn't quite forget the frightening, plastic smile and his violently bloodshot eyes.

At sixteen, several years later, you couldn't help but feel a perhaps unjustified but very real anger toward your mother's parents for never doing a damn thing to help your dad when he was struggling so deeply. Which Dad knew, but Dad had politely excused himself and Henry from the pseudo-happy reunion. His in-laws had never fully accepted him having moved on with a man and would barely acknowledge Henry when they were all in the same room. They were the only people in your life you weren't out to. When you mentioned this to your dad, he sighed and said, "That's probably a good idea." Reformed Judaism had no issue with queerness in so far as Dad explained it (at least, your own temple didn't), but your grandparents clung hard to their old traditions.

"It was awesome," Noah said of the trip. His hand was still braced from when he sprained his wrist during a mock-IDF training.

"Did you feel a connection?" your grandmother asked.

You and Noah locked eyes over the table. "It was a lot of fun," Noah said evenly.

Your grandmother pursed her lips. Truly, you should have seen this coming. Even your paternal grandfather, who had practically raised you alongside your dad, was a staunch Zionist. Later, when you went to Palestine to protest the occupation a few years after undergrad, he would refuse to acknowledge you had gone. When his friends asked, he insisted you'd gone to Israel. This infuriated you, but your dad made it worse.

"Let it go," he would say.

You tried to understand. You and Noah would never know what it was like to be ripped from your families, to be forced from your homes. And yet, your family's refusal to see Israel as anything other than a safe haven astounded you.

"They're killing Palestinians the same way the Nazis killed the Jews," you said to your dad one night as you helped him put away the dishes.

"I know, schatz." He never engaged in the conversation on either side. When you, fresh out of undergrad and visiting your dad for the week, asked him if he still did Israel Day at the temple, he wouldn't look you in the eye when he said, "The parents got angry when I tried to stop it." Just the fact that he had tried to end the annual celebration at all was the most you'd ever heard him take a side.

You had never felt a connection with Israel, nor Judaism. If you hadn't feared it would hurt your father, you probably wouldn't have graduated Hebrew school at all. Toward the end of your time there, you skipped more weeks than not. The only reason they let you graduate is because your dad was the temple educator.

The funny thing was, when you left for undergrad a few months later, substituting suburban Westchester for a small liberal arts college in Indianapolis, you couldn't seem to help but find the other Jews. Your orientation leader. A friend of your roommate's from high school. The treasurer of Pride. You found yourself at more than one Shabbat through the Jewish Student Union, sometimes staying for hours later than your group's allotted thirty minutes in the room reserved for the holiday each week, until the next club came in and took it over. Noah, on the other hand, took no part in as much as a single service. On the phone, he told you how there were no Jews on his Tampa-based campus.

"I thought you said they had a student group."

"They did last year," Noah said. "The president graduated."

"So restart it." You held your phone away from your ear to check the time. You had to leave for class in ten minutes.

"Maybe," said Noah, even though you both knew he wouldn't. He was already struggling to adjust from your small town to being one of fifty thousand students.

It was through attending the occasional Shabbat that you connected with Jewish Voice for Peace, a left-wing anti-occupation organization, your sophomore year of undergrad. The president of your college's JSU, a young woman called Annalise, invited you to join them at a local chapter meeting with a handful of the friends you'd made through Shabbat.

You continued going after Annalise graduated the following year and through JVP, you met Bree a year out of undergrad at an anti-occupation protest. One of the organizers asked if you and Bree would be willing to hand out waters to those marching, since your then-new Crohn's meds had left you lethargic and Bree had sprained her ankle the weekend before. You sat together under the too-hot sun in the middle of July. Bree was funny, pointing out the obscene signs of the counter protesters and calling out to them until they moved. You told them about how you found your way to JVP and they told you all about the community projects they did with their Unitarian church. You somehow found yourselves talking about your families, your work, your hopes for the future, and you ended the day with sunburned shoulders and Bree's number in your phone.

You'd been dating for a year when you and Bree took a trip to New York and spent the week at your childhood home. Your bank accounts wouldn't let you stay anywhere else, quite frankly, but you weren't upset about spending the weekend with Dad and Henry. Truth be told, you missed them all the way in Indianapolis.

Dad picked you up at the airport and asked Bree polite questions until you got back to the house, where you brought your and Bree's bags up to your childhood bedroom. You smiled self-indulgently at the cork board riddled with summer camp photos and old letters before you came back downstairs and found Bree with Dad and Henry in the living room.

Bree reached for you and you took their hand. You sat beside them on the couch, your legs tucked onto the cushion, and Bree asked Henry, "Do you go to temple too?"

"Every week," Henry said with a smile. He converted when you were perhaps ten. You remember being at the ceremony with Dad and Noah and Henry's sister Abby and being so excited, even though you couldn't entirely grasp the significance of his decision. All you knew was that Henry was taking an extra step to be a part of your family, and in that moment, you loved him even more.

"Are you usually the only person of color there?" Bree asked. "I do a ton with JVP and I love it, but I feel like it's so hard to connect with other Black people." Bree's family, too, was mostly white. Bree was the youngest of three, their older sister being their white parents' biological child and her brother, the middle child, also Black and adopted. They had a hard time talking to their parents—or really any of their family aside from their brother—about race, about queerness, about anything outside of their small, Christian comfort zone. Bree rarely spoke to them and when they did, conversations were perfunctory, obligatory. When you first began staying over at each other's apartments, they were in awe of your frequent FaceTimes with Dad, Henry, and Noah.

"There are two kids who go pretty regularly who're adopted and also Chinese," Henry said. "Maybe fifteen and ... I want to say seventeen? And Char is mixed. But yeah, there aren't very many of us."

"What made you decide to convert?"

Henry shot what you and Noah used to call his "heart eyes" at Dad. "This guy," he said.

They kissed chastely and you pretended to gag. "Gross," you said, grinning.

.

The four of you spent most of your time together that week. "They're really cool," Bree insisted over and over. Though the two of you had different definitions of "cool," you were nonetheless inclined to appreciate how lucky you were to have them. Abby came by to see you and meet Bree on the third day and the three of you talked for a long time over coffee in the living room, but you also got to spend some time with your dad, just the two of you. Bree slept in one Saturday morning and Henry went to the store, so you found Dad alone when you came downstairs for breakfast that morning.

"We're out of Froot Loops," he said apologetically. Everyone in the family knew Froot Loops were your favorite when you were little. Even now, you always ate them when you visited.

You shrugged and grabbed a box of Cheerios instead. "I'm sure Henry knows to get me more at the store," you said.

"Naturally."

You poured yourself a bowl and sat across from Dad. "You seem happy," you said.

"It's these," Dad said, picking up a small orange container beside his oatmeal. You had missed them before, or else he'd put them away. He unscrewed the top and tipped a pill into the palm of his hand.

You watched with amazement as he swallowed a single, bicolored Prozac. "Is this real life?" you asked.

You and Noah had been trying to get your dad into therapy since you were teens. Dad rarely spoke about his own mental health, even though he'd put you and Noah in therapy so young. Neither did your grandfather of his, though he was more than supportive of your dad's decision regarding the two of you. Your maternal grandparents wouldn't talk about mental health at all. The rare times you discussed therapy in front of them, they would scoff and change the subject.

They didn't like anything that had to do with health, really. When you were diagnosed with Crohn's in college, a diagnosis that helped your grandfather realize he had the same illness, they sent your father half a dozen emails on diet and exercise. Henry had been especially infuriated on your behalf. You had to wonder how many people had done that to him when he'd been diagnosed with MS.

"Henry got to me finally," Dad said with a shrug.

"When was this? Why didn't you say anything?"

"A couple months ago," he said.

A couple months ago would have been around the same time Henry called you and "accidentally" let it slip that Dad was struggling to get out of bed in the morning and taking too many sleeping pills to get through the night.

Dad's mouth ticked up at the corners and he said, "Did you know I'm depressed? My psychiatrist told me."

It didn't escape you that he'd dodged your second question, but you let it slide. It was enough, for now, that he made the effort to get better.

You rolled your eyes and said, "Well I could have told you that."

The following week, you brought the conversation up with your own therapist, a woman named Jeannine in her late thirties and whom you had started seeing just a few weeks before your dad must have started therapy. Jeannine always wore her hair back in a long braid and pink, square-framed glasses.

"Your dad was reluctant to accept his diagnosis," she said. "Why do you think that was?" He revealed to you later that his diagnosis had really been dual depression and PTSD. Which, duh.

"My grandpa is a Holocaust survivor," you said, "and a bunch of us have autoimmune diseases in the family. Whenever my brother or I would bring it up he was always like, you know, 'I can't have PTSD because at least I didn't live in 1940s Germany' or 'I'm not sick,' and it was obviously because Henry has MS and his dad and I have Crohn's, you know?"

"You were pretty reluctant to accept your own diagnosis," Jeannine reminded you. You had been officially diagnosed with anxiety and PTSD earlier that year.

"Yeah, I didn't think I could have been so affected by what happened to my mom. I mean, of course she died when I was a kid, but I didn't, like, see her die. Like, my dad was *there*." You paused. "Oh."

"What, oh?" Jeannine asked.

"You're really going to make me say it?"

"I don't presume to know what you're thinking," Jeannine said, crossing her legs in front of her.

You sighed. "I did the same thing he does. I 'it-wasn't-that-bad-ed' my mental health." You still did that, sometimes. When you thought of your dad or even of Roni, who you kept in touch with via email. You were working on that. Your therapist told you constantly that trauma isn't a contest, and you knew what she meant, but it was still hard to think of yourself as worthy of such a diagnosis.

Noah was, if anything, more astounded than you were when he was diagnosed with the same conditions. "I guess it all makes sense," he said over the phone. "Do you remember when we had that school shooting drill and I was fucking hysterical?"

You, who were procrastinating setting up a then-new apartment by talking to Noah, crossed your legs on the couch and said, "Oh god, Dad was so pissed. He laid into the principal and everything." Wanda, a kitten at the time, played with a catnip mouse on the floor.

"Honestly, he was right though," Noah said. "Like if my kid ever had a shooting drill and I didn't know about it, I'd be so mad." In fact, when Hallie started school several years from that conversation, it was something Noah spoke to the teacher about.

"It's so scary now," you said. Shootings were in the news all the time. A flash of screaming children and the perpetrator's mug shot before everyone forgot about it a few weeks later. Whenever the news was on when you were visiting New York, Dad would change it.

"I don't know how Dad functioned," Noah said.

"Badly," you said, but that wasn't entirely fair. Dad had been depressed and lost and broken, especially before Henry, but you wouldn't have traded him for the world. In all your years being his daughter, you never doubted for a moment that he loved you.

—

Your niece had been attending online Hebrew school for nearly three months when Hanukkah crept up on you. Tentatively, Dad asked you and Noah if you would hop on a Zoom call to light the candles for the first night, a request to which you responded affirmatively before frantically texting your friend, Riley, to see if they had a menorah you could borrow.

The first night, a few months before the Lauren Wolf fiasco, you and your family reunited on your screens just as the sun began to dip below the horizon. In Indianapolis, at least. In New York, the sun had already set, leaving the windows in Dad and Noah's backgrounds pitch black.

For all their JVP activism, Bree had never celebrated a Jewish holiday before.

"Oh god," you realized once on the call, "I haven't done the prayers in years. I don't even know if I'll remember them."

"I'll teach you," Henry teased. So many years ago, you had been the one to teach Henry the prayers. You'd insisted on being the one to do so, in fact.

Dad nudged Henry with his shoulder. "She knows them," he said.

"I really don't know if I do."

"They'll come back to you," Dad said calmly. "Ready?" You nodded and Noah said, "Yep." Your dad struck a match and you and Noah flicked on your lighters, and you began the prayers you hadn't said since you were a child:

Baruch atah Adonai
Eloheinu melech ha-olam
asher kid'shanu b'mitzvotav
v'tsivanu l'hadlik ner
shel Hanukkah.

Chapter Seven: The Ends of Us
1922-1998

The Americans liberated the camps, but they did little else. In the aftermath of Eli regaining his so-called freedom, he sat against the backdrop of barbed wire fences and military tanks, watching lost children scream for their parents and desperate parents do the same for their children. Eli didn't have the energy to scream. His head swam, blurring the scene before him of blank-faced soldiers passing out threadbare blankets to shivering figures huddled on the ground. His stomach ached with gnawing hunger and he tried to remember the last time he ate something.

Vaguely, he wondered if his sons could be among the wailing, until he remembered they would be older now, Albert fourteen and Fritz a man at eighteen. He filed these thoughts away for later, when he had food in his body and therefore energy to mourn the childhood he never got to give his own kids. They would be strangers to him now, five years of their lives gone by. Had they been taken, or had they escaped? Did they believe him dead? How would he even begin to find them?

Later, Eli would scarcely remember the long journey home. He would only recall the deep exhaustion in his bones, the embarrassment at his skeletal appearance and his broken Polish. He managed to catch a ride on the back of a cargo train with half a dozen other passengers headed back to Germany. He fell asleep for the hours-long journey, head resting against a wooden box. He woke only when prodded by the driver.

"We're here," the man said in German, and Eli lifted his weary head. His temple ached where it had pressed against the box. The others he'd come with had disembarked on the platform already, staring at the street as though in disbelief. None of them seemed to know where to begin either.

The train station was minutes from his childhood home, the home he'd become a man in, the home where he'd said goodbye to his sister and his mother before he knew it was goodbye for good, although he knew his forced departure couldn't be far into the future. His friends used to play by this station, in the field just around the corner. Later, when Eli courted Susan and after they wed, they had boarded on this very platform each time they visited Susan's parents in Hungary.

The structure hadn't changed much over the years, but Eli didn't think he'd ever seen it so quiet. "Danke," Eli murmured. He disembarked clumsily, nearly falling onto the tracks. The other man didn't offer to help him. None of the other passengers seemed to be looking at him.

He started off down the road to the home he once shared with his wife and sons, pausing every so often to catch his breath. Most likely, his family had fled or been taken, but perhaps one of his neighbors would know where. It was a start, at least. Otherwise, Eli didn't know what else to do with himself. He had no purpose now. The Nazis had taken that away along with everything else.

The once twenty-minute walk took him much longer, or he guessed it was longer. Eli didn't have a way to tell the time, but he felt each second in the ache of his joints, in the pain of the underfed muscles that hadn't walked so long in years. He passed the street he'd grown up on after fifteen minutes or so, passed the house he grew up in, window frames hanging from their hinges. Even if she had stayed, his mother wouldn't have been allowed to keep the house. He passed the Rosenbaums' place next door, though they had moved long before the war. The church that used to be at the end of the block was now a skeletal structure, burned black. No smoke. The fire had happened long ago.

At last, he arrived at the jarringly familiar home, still a pale brown with a small dirt rectangle in the front where Susan had once planted a vegetable garden. An upstairs light flickered and Eli swallowed hope he couldn't afford. Most likely someone else lived here now. It had been four years since he'd last graced his own doorstep, four years since he last held his wife and children.

Eli knocked hesitantly and listened. He imagined he could hear the squeak of the top step they never fixed however many times they told themselves they would, the slight "thump" of wood against wall as someone walked into the kitchen from living room and let the door fly too far, as Albert almost always did in his youth. Really, all he could hear was the hum of a passing car. Longing was a powerful drug.

The front door swung open and for a moment, time stood still. The woman in the entryway was the same one who'd graced Eli's rare good dreams on so many frozen nights in the camps, the same one he'd prayed to see for half a decade. And yet, she was so different. Her blonde ponytail was streaked with gray and her eyes were underlined with deep circles. Susan stepped forward and reached for him with a shaking hand.

"Eli?"

There were no words. He couldn't answer. Instead, Eli fell to his knees onto the doorstep, spent. He buried his face in his dirt-streaked hands and sobbed, overwhelmed and afraid to look too closely at the woman he was sure he imagined standing there should she fade into the ether, proving him right.

She didn't fade, though. Susan wrapped her arms around him, held him with strength Eli no longer possessed, and whispered in his ear, "It's all right, engel. It's ok. It's ok. You're home."

Susan explained everything to him over hot tea and toast in their peeling kitchen. After the SS took Eli, his mother's first priority was to protect the rest of the family. She sent Gabi and Wally to the States. Susan sent Fritz with them.

"I had to send him away," she said before Eli could even ask. "I had to keep him safe."

"I understand," he said, even though he didn't. How could she send their son away? How were they to find him again? He swallowed his devastation and did his best to take Susan at her word. He didn't have the energy to argue with her.

"I had to keep him safe," she said again, wiping a stray tear from the corner of her eye. "I didn't know what else to do."

"He wouldn't have been safe with you?" He didn't mean it as angrily as he said it, or maybe he did. His son, his firstborn, lost to them, perhaps forever.

"You don't know what it was like." Susan closed her eyes and said, "That isn't what I meant."

Eli very nearly placed a hand on hers, then withdrew. His fingers were so bony, skeletal. Susan, too, had lost weight, but not to the same extent as Eli, who was far too many harsh angles and sharp joints. He settled his hands in his lap and listened.

Susan and Albert had fled to Budapest, where they'd lived with Susan's parents. As soon as she heard the Americans were on their way to liberate the camps, she returned to Germany to wait for Eli. "I knew you would come," she said. Her eyes shined with tears that refused to fall.

"Albert?"

"He's with my parents," she said. "I didn't know ... the state of our home ..."

The state of Eli.

"I understand," Eli said again, and this time, he had begun to in earnest. This time, he took Susan's warm hands in his and tried not to think about the way he could see his bones under his skin. Her eyes were beautiful and blue and wet. "I can't believe you're here," he said. His chest loosened for the first time in four years and he took a moment to identify the foreign warmth building in his chest, in spite of everything, as a joyful anticipation in the face of seeing Albert in the not-so-distant future, as pure ecstasy in being reunited with the woman he loved and thought he may never see again. Against all odds, that feeling in his chest was hope.

.

She made him wait before they took the trip.

"You need to regain your strength," Susan said, though Eli wasn't sure how he would regain something that he no longer had. He slept the days away, waking occasionally in a fit of screaming, his limbs twisted in the sheets, convinced he lay not in his own bed but in a thin barrack pressed up against three other men. Susan would hold him as he howled in the night, make him his former favorite meals when he woke, and sit with him in the small bathroom when the rich food was too much for his shrunken stomach.

"Where do we go from here?" he asked her one night. The same old dreams had woken him at an ungodly hour and he lay in the dark holding his wife, their legs overlapping under the threadbare covers.

Even Eli wasn't entirely sure what he meant. How do we start the journey to Budapest, maybe? Or how do we move on when everything we know has been ripped out from under us? Susan took the question literally. This was, perhaps, easier for them both.

"We return to our son," she said. "And then we find the rest of our family."

—

It was easier, when speaking about everything that happened, to write it out, to have it written down. Otherwise, Eli would spend far too much time in his old age thinking not of the travel, of new places to explore and favorite haunts to revisit, but of the stomach-churning, bone-aching trauma of his first months—years really, perhaps decades—after the camps. As much as he loved, now, to share his story with generations that he hoped would never know the horrors of his youth, he had learned, in the many years past, what he could and could not tolerate.

But he did love the speaking. The traveling too. In the last four decades or so, Eli had traveled all over the world, from neighboring Romania (four hours in the car to Mişca) to Uganda (a ten-hour flight to Entebbe) and everywhere in between. Anywhere people were interested in hearing his story. As it turned out, that was a lot of places. In his youth, he had never gone far from home, never left Germany for good until he was forced. As an old man, he'd been farther than he could have fathomed all those years ago.

He had his routine now. His agent would book him a flight (window seat), a hotel (Marriott or Hilton if they had it), and book a series of talks (with enough time to tour the locale if he'd never been before). Then, Eli would phone the school or temple or community center gracious enough to host him and thank them for their time. Last, he'd do some research on the place, the Jewish community, and possibly the tourist attractions before he had to board his flight and set off for whatever new adventure awaited.

This time, Eli had skipped the research. This time, Eli was New York-bound. He'd been now at least a dozen times over the last few years alone. Albert would drive up from Maryland on day three and spend a few hours with Eli before dropping him off at the airport and making the return trip. Al had grown up to look startlingly like his mother, with soft blond hair and wide eyes. Fritz, for the first fourteen years of his life at least, had always looked more like Eli. When Eli imagined what Fritz looked like now, he could only imagine a younger version of himself.

"Why don't you come up earlier?" Eli had asked Al when they made the plans. "You can stay in my room."

"Maddy's in a play this weekend," Al told him. "Julia would kill me if I missed it." Julia was Al's daughter, Maddy his grand-daughter. More than once, Al and his wife had asked Eli to move to the States to be closer to them, especially since Susan passed four years earlier. But as much as he loved his family, as much as he had grown to love adventure, Eli couldn't bear the thought of leaving his home for good, not again. He missed his son so much it hurt, but he couldn't leave the place he'd loved his wife for most of their lives together. Hungary, not Germany. Not what they had planned.

On the flight into LaGuardia, Eli sat beside a young mother and her five- or six-year-old daughter. They were obviously American from their accents and coming back from visiting family in Budaörs based on their quiet conversation. When the mother fell asleep shortly after ordering a chicken dinner from the stewardess, the girl busied herself with a well-loved *Calvin and Hobbes* comic and quickly found herself stuck on page six.

After she'd been frowning at the page for several minutes, Eli looked over her shoulder at the page and the girl caught his gaze.

"I don't know this word," she said. She pointed to the speech bubble above Calvin's head.

"It says 'habitat,'" Eli said.

"What's that mean?"

"See the pond?" he asked. He pointed at the panel on the opposite page, where Calvin and Hobbes stood in front of a small body of water. "That would be a habitat for frogs or fish. A home."

The girl's eyes wandered up Eli's forearm and settled on his faded tattoo. "My Mema has numbers here," she said, rubbing her own forearm. "Were you in the Holocaust too?"

Once upon a time, such a question would have jarred him. Now, he only smiled at the girl as he patiently explained his history. Their shared history, from what she'd shared of her relative.

"I was in Auschwitz during the Second World War," he said. "I'm a survivor."

The first time someone asked Eli to speak about his time in the camps, he was astounded. His rabbi approached him and asked if he'd like to tell his story to the congregation's older children.

"It's not a happy story, rabbi," Eli said. In the five years since he'd moved to Hungary he had become fluent in the language, but every word he spoke felt heavy on his tongue. This was a language he shouldn't have needed to learn.

"I know," Rabbi Molnár said. "But it is an important one for them to know. Many of them are too young to remember how devastating it was."

The thought shook Eli to his core. One day, there would be people who didn't remember. That would be wonderful for them, and terrifying. "I need to think about it," Eli said.

That night, he went to Susan. They lay under the covers together like they had back in Germany in the nights after Eli came home. Susan combed her fingers through his hair in an attempt to keep him grounded, away from bad memories.

"Is this something you want to do?" she asked.

"I don't know," Eli said. "I know it's important. I know that."

"But you don't have to be the one to tell them."

Eli sighed. He'd thought this too, in a moment of self-pity and quite frankly, anger. Why him? Was he to relive the press of sticky and shaking bodies on the way to Krakow, the sting of the tattoo needle bleeding blue ink onto his skin against his will, the way his arms burned after so many days of fueling the war effort of the Nazis, every day for the rest of his life? Should he open his chest and lay his heart bare for young minds to examine as a history lesson? The one thing that kept him from rejecting the offer entirely was the fear that everyone else would think the same, that no one would tell these new generations what their ancestors had survived.

He ran a hand over his face and repeated what he said to the rabbi: "I need to think about it."

In the end, Eli agreed to Rabbi Molnár's request, though he very nearly pulled out again the night before.

"I can't do this," he said to Susan between sobs, his wet face buried in her neck. He'd lost count of the number of times he'd done this, broken down completely in Susan's arms while she waited patiently for him to come back to himself, to come back to her.

"You can," she said fiercely. "Eli, I don't know anyone braver than you."

The day of the talk, he stumbled over his words and struggled to look the crowd of teens in their eager faces. A year ago, Albert might have been among them, but his son was at university now, studying history not far from home. At first, Eli and Susan went to see him every weekend, until Susan protested that they had to let him go eventually. Eli still found himself plagued by bouts of nausea-inducing anxiety on the weekends they didn't see their son.

After the talk, Eli locked himself in the temple bathroom and cried again. He cried for himself and for his mother and for his sister and for his son, and because he didn't know what to do now that he knew speaking so freely to a couple dozen young faces who genuinely wanted to hear his story made him feel lighter than he had in nearly ten years.

———

A woman in the front row of the crowd at Temple Beth Shalom in Great Neck raised a gloved hand and Eli pointed to her around the microphone stand from his place at the front of the synagogue. It was Eli's second talk since arriving in New

York yesterday, his second of four he would give on this trip. The woman cleared her throat, thanked him for his words, and asked, "Were you ever able to find your sister and son?"

"No," Eli said into the mic. "We tried everything. My younger son even took a DNA test in the hopes Fritz had done so as well. We did not get any results." The woman deflated in her seat, and Eli wished he could tell her differently. It was a common question and it didn't hurt the way it used to. Nonetheless, the dull ache for the son he'd lost lingered in his chest, never quite leaving him, nor would he want it to.

After the questions, which ran several minutes late, several of the congregants stayed behind to thank him, to shake his hand, to tell him their own stories. Eli loved this part, truly, but he'd be lying if he said he didn't want to head back to his hotel and sleep for the next three days. He was an old man, after all. The traveling exhausted him in a way it didn't used to.

He politely excused himself and made for the door when he heard a faint, "Mr. Altenberg?" Eli turned and found himself looking at the same woman he'd been avoiding all evening.

Not her fault. He never met this woman before and didn't know anything about her now except that she'd sat in the third row toward the middle aisle and appeared to be accompanied by a little boy with dark brown skin and curly hair he kept pushing out of his eyes.

But even now, decades removed from the last time he saw his sister, he saw her and Fritz everywhere he went. He would be out in a crowd and cease to breathe as he saw Gabi's ponytail swish ahead of him, only to remember Gabi would be an old woman by now. At talks, he would spot Fritz's young face in the crowd, only to blink and realize the young boy in the fourth row was taller, paler, and not at all the same boy Eli had been searching for all these decades.

The woman before him wore her dark hair the same way Gabi used to, had the same wrinkle in her forehead Eli remembered from when Gabi was a young girl frustrated with her subtraction homework. The boy with her stood a half a step back.

"Hello," Eli said evenly. "Thank you so much for coming."

"Of course," the woman said. "I'm Rebecca and this is Jason. Thank you for sharing your story." She hesitated for a moment. "I just had to ask," she said, "was your sister's name Gabi Keefer, by any chance?"

—

Before they took him, before his family scattered like winter-weakened leaves in a storm, Eli knew things were about to change for the devastating. He and many of his friends lost their jobs. The whole family took to rationing what little they could afford. The day the Third Reich announced the demarcation of Jews by yellow armband, Eli went to see his mother.

Her eyes were underlined with heavy bags and her disheveled hair had been thrown back into a messy ponytail, but when she hugged him tight it felt the same, despite her smaller frame. She felt strong and soft and warm. She felt the same as she did when Eli, at six years old, fell and scraped his knee in the street and she scooped him up in her arms, even though he was far too big to be carried like that. She felt like the day his father died and she held him close and told him, even though she must have been aching with loss, that they were going to be ok, and Eli couldn't help but believe her because if Mama said it, it must be true. In her arms, Eli felt at home.

They sat at the kitchen table holding hands to keep them from shaking. It wasn't a weekend, but the Shabbat candles were already out, or else still out. It took too much energy to put them away each time.

"They're coming for us," Eli said.

Mama nodded. "Yes," she said.

Eli ran a hand through his curly hair. "They'll come for the men first," he said. "If I can't escape, save my sons. However you can."

"I will," Mama said softly.

"They'll be safe in Hungary. Susan can say they're fully Hungarian."

"I'll tell her."

"You can leave with Gabi," he said. "She'll need you. Run. Maybe ..."

"Eli," she interrupted. "Do you really think if they took you I'd be able to leave?"

Eli's mouth hung open for a moment before he gathered his thoughts. "You can't ... You can't mean you'll stay," he practically shouted. "Mama, they'll kill us."

"I know," Mama said, moving a frail hand to Eli's cheek. "But if anything happened to you or Gabi, I wouldn't be able to go on anyway."

.

That Friday, Eli came back with his wife and sons for Shabbat, the last before they would put him on an overcrowded train to Krakow. Fritz and Al were unusually quiet (especially unusual for Al) as they walked to Eli's mother's house. People kept their heads down, their pace quick. No one looked at Eli and his family, even those Eli considered friends just a year prior, but not because they didn't notice them. No one wanted to be associated with a Jewish family anymore.

Gabi and Wally were already at the house when Eli, Susan, and the boys arrived. Their faces were pained and both of them were far too thin, though nowhere near as thin as Eli would become. Eli hugged his sister and wished her good Shabbos.

"You look beautiful," he lied. She smiled at him, and Eli committed that smile to memory, just in case. It was one of the few things that gave him hope in the camps, that he would see that smile again.

After, when he failed and failed and failed to find her, that smile burned into his brain became a burden, a constant reminder of all he had lost. He hated that, that the greatest gift his sister had given him had become too agonizing to touch.

—

The woman who claimed to be his niece made a quick phone call and came back with the little boy. "She's didn't answer," the woman said. "She's probably asleep."

"That's all right," Eli lied. He struggled to keep the disappointment from turning his smile. He'd forgotten how late it was, and Gabi was always one to go to sleep early. As a child, she would wake with the sunrise, only a few hours after Eli had gone to bed in the first place. He was torn between amazement that that one small thing had stayed the same and utter disappointment that this nearly unbelievable miracle hadn't come to fruition. For a brief moment, he really believed he would see sister that night.

"I'll call her first thing tomorrow," the woman said.

"Of course." Not "the woman." Rebecca. His niece's name was Rebecca. It was a beautiful name. Perhaps named for their mother, Ruth. He would have to ask Gabi if (when, please be when) he saw her at last.

"Is there a number I can call to reach you?" Rebecca asked.

Eli jotted the hotel number on the small yellow pad he carried and tore out the page. "If I'm not there, I will be at a talk," he said. "You can leave a message."

"Fantastic," Rebecca beamed at him. Gabi's smile, radiant and slightly gapped. The smile his sister had gifted him on their last Shabbat.

"Can I hug you?" Eli asked. He hadn't meant to say it. The words slipped past his lips in a moment of desperation, the need to hold Gabi's daughter in his arms. Rebecca nodded and must have said something like "sure" or "of course" and he hugged her close to him, deceptively strong for ninety, as though his body were making up for all those years lost in the camps.

.

It took ages for Eli to get to sleep that evening. He dreamed not of Gabi, who often haunted his dreams, nor of his mother, nor of his wife. He dreamed of Goldie Rosenbaum.

From the time he was born, Eli grew up next to the Rosenbaums: Goldie, her parents, and her younger brother, Max. Goldie was a year above Eli, his first friend and his guide once he got to school. She was always just Goldie, just the girl who lived next door, until Eli, at the age of thirteen or fourteen, began to notice just how soft her hair looked in the morning light on their walks to school or how her crooked smile made his stomach swirl with overeager butterflies. He began to wonder what it would feel like to hold her hand.

The first time Goldie kissed him, he was fifteen and she sixteen. They'd been down by the creek, walking along the water on their way home from the first day back to school in comfortable silence, when Goldie took his arm, her hand warm on his skin as she spun him around. She stood on her toes to reach Eli's lips with hers, and Eli melted into her touch, the unexpected feel of her mouth on his sending chills up his arms. Her lips were just as soft as her hair.

Goldie broke the kiss and took a step back. "Um. I've been wanting to do that for a while," she admitted. When Eli only stared at her, dumbfounded, she tucked her hair behind her ears and asked, "Was that ok?"

Eli nodded and reached across the small gap between them to cup her face. Goldie's eyes fluttered shut, her lashes brushing against the pads of Eli's thumbs. Eli pulled Goldie closer to him once more and kissed her again, and again, and again. His heart pounded against his rib cage, sounding out the syllables of her name in his chest. *Gold-ie. Gold-ie. Gold-ie.*

Eli had very nearly forgotten, upon returning home, that this was Gabi's first day of kindergarten. He'd quite frankly forgotten how to act, in the last half hour or so, around anyone who wasn't Goldie. He sat across from Gabi at the kitchen table, stuffed one of their mother's rolls into his mouth, and asked her about her day.

Gabi took a small bite of her the roll on her plate. "Good," she said. "I got a boyfriend."

Eli hadn't meant to laugh, but the news from his five-year-old sister caught him off guard. He very nearly choked on his roll. "You're moving a little quick there, aren't you?" he asked. "First day and everything." He didn't think he'd even looked at a girl until he'd noticed Goldie.

"I don't know," Gabi said with a shrug. "His name is Wally, and I love him." Love was in the air that day, it seemed. Eli grinned in spite of himself.

Mama followed them into the kitchen and leaned over to kiss Eli on his head. "It's true," she said, shooting a knowing look at Eli. "We'll be hearing wedding bells soon." Gabi turned her head, and Mama shot him a wink.

．

That evening, after she had put Gabi to bed with a story, Mama came into Eli's room. "Is there something you'd like to tell me?" she asked, leaning against the doorframe.

Eli tore his gaze away from the window, through which he could see Goldie's house. He shook his head. "No," he said. "Nothing."

Mama sat at the edge of the bed. "Really?" she asked, smiling to herself. "You're very happy today."

Eli shrugged and Mama said, "Mr. Blauner saw you holding hands with Goldie after school."

So, he'd been found out. He couldn't seem to make himself care much, though, and he certainly couldn't stop the grin spreading slowly over his face. "She kissed me," Eli said softly.

"I knew it," Mama said, grinning too as she smoothed Eli's hair away from his face. "You and Gabi can have a joint wedding."

Eli rolled his eyes affectionately. "Next week might be too soon for me," he said. "Gabi moves fast."

"I'm happy for you, schatz," Mama said with a laugh. "I hope she makes you happy."

Eli nodded. "She does," he said. "She really does."

．

Eli promised Goldie that they'd marry, perhaps the following summer. They could do it by the creek, the spot where they'd first gotten together.

Instead, she broke the news to him in that same spot. Goldie sat on a rock, her captivating eyes red-rimmed and her lower lip trembling. Eli couldn't quite believe her at first.

"You won't be leaving forever," he said. "You'll come back, won't you?"

"Eli, we are. We're leaving." Goldie took a slow, shaky breath. "You could come with us," she said. "We could marry in America."

Slowly, Eli shook his head. He could never leave Mama or Gabi, not even for the young woman he so badly wanted to spend forever with.

"Why do you have to leave at all?" he asked, even though he knew. Even then, he and Goldie had been called a series of slurs walking in town together. Mr. Rosenbaum had seen a sharp dive in his business over the last few years.

"Please, Eli. I don't want to lose you."

Eli looked around him, as though the answer would come to him in this clearing they both loved. "My whole family is here," he said.

Goldie nodded. "They could come too," she said. "My aunt and uncle have a large house. We would figure it out."

Eli's eyes welled with tears too. "I'm so sorry, Goldie."

She leaned forward and kissed him, clinging to the front of his shirt and hungrily pressing their mouths together. Eli rose to his knees and kissed her back with equal fierceness, with longing and with fear. He pressed into those kisses all the words he could not say. His heartbreak. His fear for his own family, whom he knew wouldn't leave Germany until they were forced.

The day she left, Eli came to her house to say goodbye. They took a stroll only to the end of the block and back before it was time for the Rosenbaums to leave. He sobbed all that night, and his mother held him like she used to when he was Gabi's age.

"Why did she have to leave?" he asked her, even though the answer hadn't changed. "I could have protected her."

"Oh, Eli," his mother said, pressing a gentle kiss along the part in his hair. She didn't say what she was thinking then, but in the dream, Eli knew. He couldn't protect Goldie. He couldn't even protect himself.

—

As Eli woke from the memory (more and more of his dreams were memories as he got older) and all the following morning, he thought of the ones he'd lost. Goldie, the one the war took first, weaved her way through his thoughts during both talks, forcing him to pause at odd moments, though his audiences likely attributed this to age. He tripped over Mama's name in his telling of his story, the ache of his longing for her sharper than it had been in years. And of course, he couldn't stop thinking how maybe, just maybe, he would see his sister today for the first time in over fifty years, and about how broken he would be if he didn't.

He got back to the hotel at just after two o'clock to find a message for him at the front desk with a number to dial should he want to speak with a Mrs. Gabi Keefer. Eli made the phone call from his room, breathing deeply as it rang. Perhaps she wouldn't answer, or perhaps it had all been a mistake. Perhaps there was another Gabi Keefer living in New York who'd lost her brother in the devastation of the Holocaust. It was a common name, theirs a common story. Eli hadn't even called Al yet to tell him the news in case this all turned out to be a terrible misunderstanding.

"Hello?"

Time stopped. The voice on the other end of the phone was older, softened by years of speaking American English, but he would recognize it anywhere.

In German, Eli answered, "Is that really you, Gabi?"

After a fuzzy beat in which he worried she would tell him no, this had all been a horrible and heart-wrenching mistake, Gabi spoke in the same language.

"Oh God," she said, "Eli. My Eli. My brother."

———

A year after Eli made it to Hungary, Otto Tolle's parents tracked him down. Otto had been a friend of Gabi's decades ago, from the time they were children to the time the SS took Eli away to the camps. Otto's parents sent a letter with a brief note to say Eli's mother had written after Otto had already been caught smuggling Jews out of Germany. They wrote how proud they were, and how he had been killed three days before the letter arrived. At last, they could give the letter to Ruth's son.

Eli read,

Dear Otto,

Considering everything that has happened in the last few years, I do not know how to start this letter. What do you say to a young man you haven't spoken to in several years while the world falls apart around you both? How does one communicate their deepest fears, their desires, the burdens they are about to place on another? I do hope you and your family are doing well. The last I spoke with your parents, your younger sisters had both been attending university and your brother had just had a daughter! They were so proud of all of you, Otto, the last time we saw each other. This was over two years ago, however, and these days, even doing well seems to be a rather large ask. Long before I went into hiding, we were scraping by for food, and I imagine it is much of the same everywhere, though perhaps they feed you well in the army. I do hope so, as I hate the idea of you going hungry. Which brings me to why I am writing this letter: Otto, the people I am with have told me you could possibly help me, that you have helped dozens already escape death at the hands of the Nazis. I feel truly terrible asking for your assistance when I can give you nothing in return. I do hope that, in the future, I will be able to return the favor. I love to imagine a time in which this is possible, in which I will be able to speak with you face to face. Perhaps such a thing is futile, but in spite of everything, I have hope.

How strange it is that I knew you when you were so young, and now you are a soldier, dear Otto, and continuing to do what is right despite the danger you must face. I cannot reconcile the image of you in uniform with that of the young, cherubic boy with perpetually pink cheeks and a love for bienenstich, who was such good friends with my Gabi. Do you remember when you two first met? Probably not, as you were so young. I was delighted to learn that there was a young couple living down the street, especially after the early death of my beloved husband, with a son my daughter's own age. You and Gabi were fast friends, and I was not at all surprised when it was you she chose to marry her and Wally on the playground all those years ago. Do you remember that day? She came home so excited, sure she and Wally would be together forever. I laughed, sure she would move on within the month. That just goes to show you even mothers are wrong sometimes, doesn't it? But I digress. As such a good friend of the family, I am sure you remember my son and Gabi's older brother, Eli, who was one of the first to be taken to the internment camps when the SS began rounding us up and hauling us away. Otto, you cannot even imagine the pain of hearing your firstborn has been taken to work for these monsters who would have him dead. I cried day and night after they took him, but of course I had to keep it together for my Gabi. She and Wally have escaped, as have Eli's wife, Susan, and his sons, Fritz and Albert (I won't say to where in case this letter is intercepted), but I am determined to find my son and bring him home. Gabi did ask me to come with her, but how can I leave now when half my heart is still held captive?

Unlike the rest of my family, then, I am still in Germany, as I will not leave while my son is still lost to me. Again, I cannot say where I am staying should this letter be intercepted. If only I could tell you everything! Alas, I do not want the kind people who have helped me to get into trouble after they have done so much. I hope you never know the fear of being hunted, of knowing in the eyes of so many that you are less than human just because of where you pray and the holidays you hold dear. The kind people here have promised to post this letter on my behalf. Unfortunately, there is no way you will be able to reply, but it is no matter. All I ask of you, Otto, is that you try your best to bring my Eli home.

Remembering the little things brings me the rare moment of joy, now. I sit in the small space which I now occupy and I smile as I remember the warmth of Eli's gaze when I tucked him into bed at night to tell him a story or the joy I felt watching Gabi and you and all your friends playing your secret spies game in our back yard. Do you remember that time? It seems so long ago now, almost like a dream. In looking back, at the very least, I know I was a good mother. I see Eli's children in my mind's eye and I am so unbelievably proud that I raised a son who would make such an incredible father. I remember Gabi on her wedding day wearing the dress I wore to my own wedding and can't help grinning to myself in this little, dusty corner I now occupy. She was so beautiful that day, wouldn't you agree? Of course, my Gabi was always beautiful. Even the last few times I saw her, when she had lost weight and could only afford to wash her hair once a week, she was the most beautiful woman I've ever seen. She takes after her father, you know. Both my children do. Marcel, too, had the same thick eyebrows and lashes, the same dark, shining eyes I fell in love with when I was not much younger than Gabi is now. Marcel adored his children both and was lost to us too soon, though perhaps, now, it is for the best. I cannot imagine he would be able to bear what has happened to our family.

Could you possibly do one more thing for me? Could you ensure you, too, stay safe whilst helping my people? It is perhaps selfish to ask such a thing of you when I know how important it is that you do this work, but I cannot stand the thought of losing someone my daughter held so dearly, or losing a son, a brother, and a good man. I cannot stand the thought of losing one more person I love.

Have faith, dear Otto. Much love,
Ruth Altenberg

Eli folded the letter against his chest and breathed. In. Out. In. Out. The way he did so often these last few months, since reuniting with Susan and Albert, to avoid breaking down completely. He struggled too often against moments of blinding panic, with memories that crept up on him and threatened to strangle him when he least expected it. When he took walks with his son or curled up in bed with his wife.

Secret spies. He remembered that game. He remembered watching Gabi and her friends pass notes back and forth in the yard thinking they were so clever for thinking of their secret code. The first letters of each sentence spelled a word. In his mother's case, the first letter of every paragraph. The church that had been a pile of rubble and ash when Eli caught a glimpse of it after coming home, that must have been the church that attempted to shield his mother. Had she been caught in the fire? Had she been taken before the church burned? He would never know, and how could he be ok with that?

He held the last words his mother had perhaps ever written and forced himself to think not of the agony of their separation, of her waiting endlessly and faithfully for him to come back to her, but of his love for her, for his family. He thought of the first time he laid eyes on Gabi. She had screamed as soon as he entered the room and Mama, still exhausted from the birth, gave a half-laugh.

Papa howled and teased, "She likes you already." He threw an arm around Eli's thin shoulders as Eli grinned. He'd been asking for a sibling for years, even though Mama and Papa were open with him about how hard it had been to get pregnant. He knew about the miscarriages and he mourned for them, but he had never stopped hoping. And now here she was, his sister. Gabriella.

"I love her," Eli said.

His mother cupped his chin in her hand. "I knew you would," she said. "You know you have a job as her older brother, yes? This is your baby sister, Eli. You will have to keep her safe."

Eli nodded, still smiling. Gabi looked up at him and her lips twisted into something like a smile. He chose to believe it was, anyway. He looked back at his mother, who even in her exhaustion delighted in her children's joy.

"I will, Mama."

—

Eli took a cab to Gabi's house in Brooklyn. His leg shook with nervous energy the whole way, a habit he'd developed after the war. The driver pulled up in front of a pale blue two-story house with a gold number three on the dark wood door. Eli thanked him and paid. He knocked just below the number and waited only a moment before the door flew open.

It amazed him how his sister looked so familiar and so foreign all at once. Her formerly long, dark hair was shoulder length and entirely iron gray, but it fell in the same beautiful waves. A web of lines decorated the delicate skin around her deep, dark eyes. She had lost height, or else she stooped her shoulders. A tear fell from the corner of her eye, and she reached for Eli. In German she said, "My brother. You're home."

He embraced her and soon he was crying too, his tears leaking quietly into Gabi's hair. She gently pushed him back and held him at arm's length, surveying him, both of them still red-eyed.

"I can't believe you're here," she said. "You're here."

Eli took her hand. "None of this feels real." This whole day had an odd film over it, an unreality Eli couldn't quite push through. He took a deep breath and managed to stem his tears. For the moment, at least.

"Come," Gabi said, wiping at her eyes. "Everyone is waiting for you."

"Everyone?" he asked, but Gabi only took his hand and led him to the kitchen. His eyes locked on one of two men at the table, the one who even after so many decades remained hauntingly familiar. Like Gabi, he had aged, face heavy with thin lines of grief and hair silver at the temples, but Eli could see the barely-a-teenager underneath the visage of a man in his late sixties, the small boy who so shared Eli's likeness.

Eli barely managed to say the name. "Fritz?" His voice broke on the one syllable and the temporarily stilled tears broke free again.

Eli's son rose from his seat and embraced his father. "Hi, Papa."

Eli wrapped his arms around Fritz in return, scarcely daring to breathe. Any moment now, he would wake up and realize none of this was real, that his mind was playing horrible tricks on him the way it had in the years after the liberation of Auschwitz.

But it was real. Fritz pulled away and Eli raised a hand to his cheek the same way his mama used to do to him. "I thought I'd never see you again."

Fritz took Eli's hand in his and gestured to the other man at the table, the youngest of them, perhaps in his late thirties. He had Eli's face and Susan's gentle smile.

"This is my son," Fritz said. "Zane."

A grandson. His grandson. Zane stood, hand extended. "It's wonderful to meet you," he said, and Eli was delighted to know his American grandson spoke German too.

Eli grabbed his hand and pulled him in for a hug. "Zane," he repeated. "It's indescribable to meet you."

"Rebecca said you're living in Budapest," Fritz said. "How did you get here? How did you find Mama and Al?" He resumed his seat.

"That," Eli said, "is a story." He sat across from his son, beside his sister, and as the sun began to set on the most unbelievable day of Eli's life in his over ninety years, he began to tell it.

Epilogue: Ruby's Story
2020-2023

Ruby loves her new dress. It's pale blue with dark edges and it puffs out when she twirls, which she likes doing in the lobby of the hotel she's staying in with her family. It makes her feel fancy.

"Be careful," Daddy warns her as she spins again. "Don't fall."

His voice is a little muffled by his mask. Even though they all have their shots, Daddy told her she isn't allowed to take hers off until they got to Aunt Claire's because of Henry, which, duh, she knows that already. Ruby never once protested about masks or the new rules, even when the pandemic first started and she wasn't allowed to go to school anymore. She's glad to be back with her friends now though. Or, not now, since it's summer, but when the school year starts again, she'll be in fourth grade and in class with her best friend, Nat.

"I won't," Ruby huffs. She's nine years old after all. She isn't seven like Micah, who would probably fall if he tried to spin like she spins. Even if it looks like she's about to knock into the bald man in the black suit walking past them, she knows better.

"We're going to be late," Mama says, taking her hand. "You look beautiful today, Ruby."

"Thank you, Mama," she says because it's polite, even though she knows.

Mama calls a cab over and sits in the front and gives the driver directions to Aunt Claire's. Daddy sits between her and Micah. It's a quick drive and then they're pulling up to the big house Aunt Claire and Uncle Matt live in. They're Daddy's aunt and uncle, but Ruby has always called them that anyway. She gets out of the car and Daddy hands her the present on the lawn, a big box with wrapping paper left over from last Hanukkah, so it has menorahs on it even though it isn't the holiday season.

"Do you want to give this to Aunt Claire?" he asks, and Ruby nods. She likes handling the present. It makes her feel important.

The front door opens and Miranda and Noah come outside. Miranda and Noah aren't really her cousins or her aunt and uncle either, but they're some sort of cousin of Daddy's. Ruby doesn't really care. They greet her with a hug and tell her she's gotten so big since they last saw her, and she asks if they like her new dress.

"It's very pretty, Ruby," Miranda says with a smile.

"Thank you," she says again. This is exactly why Ruby loves seeing her family.

—

Ruby had just started second grade when her teacher gave her an assignment. "I have to do a family tree," she told Daddy. "Mama said to let her finish work and ask you."

Daddy laughed. Ruby missed her friends at school now that her class was online, but she liked having all day with Mama and Daddy, even if Micah annoyed her sometimes. She sat next to Daddy on the couch and put the markers and the paper on the table.

"All right," Daddy said. "Well, there's you and Micah, so you can write your names here." He pointed to the bottom of the page and Ruby made stick figure people and wrote RUBY and MICAH in capital letters. They were her favorite kind of letters.

"And then me and Mama." She made stick figure people for Daddy and Mama and connected them with a line, then she made lines going to her and Micah. Under their stick figures she wrote AYESHA and JASON, spelling the names with Daddy's help.

"Mama's parents are Farhat and Ahmed, and my parent's names are Lena and Sid," he said. Ruby drew the stick figures and wrote the names, again with Daddy's help. "How far back does this have to go?"

Ruby shrugged. "Where does Aunt Claire go?"

"Aunt Claire is my mom's sister," Daddy said, "but I don't think you need her on there." Ruby shrugged again and Daddy said, "You know, I wasn't really close with Aunt Claire growing up. I didn't see a lot of her until I was a teenager."

"Why not?"

"She and my mom weren't very close," Daddy said. "But when I moved in with Grandma Rebecca, I saw her more. Not a lot because she still lived in Maryland, but we got much closer." Ruby had never met Grandma Rebecca, but she wished she did. The way Daddy said it, it sounded like she was very nice.

"What about Miranda?" Ruby liked Miranda. Miranda always told her she was pretty. She only really saw Miranda when the whole family did things, but she wished it was more.

"Miranda is my … She's my mom's second cousin. Maybe."

"I think that's it." Ruby capped her marker. "What do you think?"

"It's amazing," Daddy said. "You're an artist." He tapped the top of the page. "Do you think it needs a title?"

Ruby thought about it, then wrote, MY FAMILY at the top of the page. That time, she spelled it all by herself. After she showed her teacher and got a (virtual) check plus on the project, Daddy and Mama hung it up on the fridge.

"Family is very important, Ruby," Mama said after they hung it. She smoothed Ruby's bangs back from her forehead and planted a gentle kiss in the center.

.

Mama and Daddy met way before Ruby was born, obviously, but they told her the story after the family tree project. Daddy was just Jason then, since Ruby and Micah didn't exist, and Mama was just Ayesha. Jason wasn't from California, but he stayed there after school because all his friends were there and he got a job there that he still had. He told Ruby it was his home now.

Mama (Ayesha) was from here. Her whole family was in California, her parents and her older sister and her younger brother. She went to grad school after college and worked at the coffee shop where Jason would go a lot before work.

"I thought he was very handsome," Mama told Ruby, "so I asked him to get dinner with me after work."

"Which you were very specifically not supposed to do," Daddy said. He was smiling, though, so even though Mama wasn't supposed to do it, it couldn't have been that bad.

Mama winked at Ruby. "He didn't have a beard then," Mama said. "So you could see his incredibly handsome dimples." Ruby and Micah had the same dimples.

"The beard makes me look distinguished," Daddy said, nudging Mama's shoulder with his.

"The rest, as they say, is history." She took Daddy's hand in hers and wound her fingers around his. Daddy kissed the back of Mama's hand.

"Ok," Ruby said. "Can I go play now?" She loved Mama and she loved Daddy, but she was kind of bored of the story and their flirting, which they did all the time. Ruby thought they flirted more and more every year.

Both her parents laughed and she didn't really understand why, but they let her go, so she supposed it didn't matter. Later, when she was playing with her dolls in her room, she decided to make them meet in a coffee shop in California, since she supposed the idea was rather romantic, even if the story wasn't very exciting.

Perhaps a few months after that, Ruby met her grandma for the first time. Not Mama's mom, her Nani, the grandma she had known her whole life and who made her chocolate cookies on the weekends sometimes and loved Ruby with her whole heart, even if she smelled like old people. Daddy's mom, someone she'd only ever heard hushed whispers about from Mama and Daddy and Aunt Claire.

Daddy asked Ruby if she wanted to meet her grandma before her grandma came to visit. "Outside?" Ruby asked. That was how she saw her friends from school since the pandemic didn't let them hang out inside.

"Yep. Good memory, Ruby." Yes, she had a very good memory. Her teacher had said so last week.

"Do you want me to meet her?" Ruby asked.

"I want you to do what you're comfortable with."

"Is this why you've been sad this week?" Daddy hadn't been willing to play with her as much or read to her at night. She thought something was wrong and she didn't know why this would be it, but Daddy's mom coming to visit was the only thing different in their lives right now, especially since they weren't able to leave the house very much.

Daddy nodded. "Yeah, Ruby."

"Why?"

He thought about it. His eyebrows furrowed, and he frowned. Ruby hoped she hadn't said anything to make Daddy sad. He rubbed the back of his neck and said, "My mom and I haven't spoken in a very long time. It's a little strange, but I think I want to see her again."

"You don't know?"

Daddy shook his head. "No," he said.

Ruby couldn't think of a reason why she shouldn't see her grandma if Daddy was doing it. Micah, too, wanted to meet her, so the two of them sat with Daddy and Mama in chairs on the lawn and waited for their grandma to come.

She pulled up in a green van and parked it next to the lawn. When she got out, Ruby saw that she had silver in her dark hair and that it was very curly, like Daddy's. She was white and her skin had wrinkles on her forehead and around her mouth. Her eyes were very blue. Ruby saw little parts of her in Daddy, like in the shapes of their mouths and how thick their eyebrows were.

Ruby's grandma stopped when she saw the whole family sitting out front and Ruby wondered what she was waiting for. Eventually, Daddy waved her over and she came and sat in the vacant fifth seat.

"Hey," Daddy said. "How was the drive?"

"Good." Grandma said. "Fine. It's not far." She was staying in a hotel. Daddy told Ruby that. Grandma used to live in New York, but now she lived in New Jersey with her new boyfriend, whom Daddy said seemed nice, but he couldn't say for sure.

"These are my kids," Daddy said. "That's Ruby and Micah." He sounded very stiff. Like a robot. Ruby would never talk to Mama that way, but she didn't think now was the time to say so.

"Hi," Grandma said. She smiled at them. It was a very small smile, and she still didn't look very happy.

"Hi," Ruby and Micah said together. "Are you visiting California?" Ruby asked.

"I'm visiting your dad," Grandma said. "I haven't seen him in a very long time."

"Why?" Ruby asked.

Grandma thought about it for a minute. "I was very, very sick for a long time, and it made me do things that hurt my family. But I'm getting better and I want to be in their lives again. If they'll let me." She looked over at Daddy, and it seemed to Ruby like Daddy was the parent and Grandma was the child, since she had to ask him if it was ok to do things, just like Ruby or Micah would. Daddy nodded, and Grandma relaxed her shoulders. She turned back to Ruby and Micah. "I'm really happy to meet you," she said. "I've wanted to meet you for a long time."

—

Even though Ruby grew up in California, just like Mama, some of her favorite times have been on the east coast. Daddy's dad lives in New York and Daddy's brother and sister, Aunt Molly and Uncle Ryan, live in Maine and Massachusetts. A lot of Daddy's family lives in New York like his dad, like Noah and

Zane and Henry. Ruby likes visiting and getting dressed up and seeing shows. Last time they were there, Ruby got to see *The Lion King* on Broadway. Aunt Claire and Uncle Matt live in Maryland, but that's fun too, even if there aren't as many shows there.

Now, it's Aunt Claire's fifty-third birthday. She was supposed to have a party for her fiftieth birthday, but then the pandemic happened and Ruby only saw her family on FaceTime for a few years. Her little cousin, James, is still little, but not as much, since he was born right before the pandemic started and obviously he isn't a baby anymore. Micah plays with Hallie usually, since she's seven too. Lydia and Sarah, who are Claire's daughters, are busy telling three-year-old James how cute he is, even though Ruby thinks she was cuter at that age. Ruby sits with Mama and Aunt Claire and Henry, who are drinking adult grape juice they say Ruby isn't allowed to have until she's older.

Ruby sits next to Aunt Claire on the couch. Mama is in the armchair, and Henry is next to her in his wheelchair. His hands shake a little bit. More than they used to, but still not that much.

"I'm glad we got to do this," Aunt Claire says. "I love my brother-in-law, but it was really hard not to see anyone else for so long."

"I think Jason feels the same way," says Mama. "Especially when the pandemic hit."

"Is he close with your parents?"

"Sure, but it's not the same, like you said."

"We've all spread out," Henry says with a smile. "We got Miranda up for Hallie's consecration when that happened though. We weren't sure we'd be able to do that."

"Matt and I were supposed to go visit Zane and Henry right before the pandemic," Aunt Claire says to Mama. To Henry she says, "And now this is the first time I've seen you guys in person in three years."

"Is your sister coming?" Mama asks. "Jason mentioned you invited her."

Aunt Claire shook her head. "No. She says she's not ready to see everyone."

"I'm sorry," Mama says.

Aunt Claire shrugs. "She seems to be doing ok," she says. "I'm happy for her, if she's really happy."

Ruby looks around the room, trying to figure out where Hallie and Micah might have wandered off to, when Uncle Matt calls everyone out to the back yard for lunch. Ruby rushes out with the other kids, past the mezuzah on the back door (they have one just like it at home, only more purple instead of green-blue) and clammers for the hot dogs on the table.

—

Ruby loved Hebrew school. She started going three years ago, when she was five. She learned how to say hello and count to twenty in Hebrew. She liked it when the rabbi told them stories. She made some of her best friends there—Emma Han and Jenny Utami. The only thing she didn't love was that her friends didn't go to school with her, even if she had Nat.

"Well," Mama told her one night over dinner, "your Hebrew school is a little far, Rubes. It wouldn't make sense for Emma and Jenny's parents to drive them all the way out here for school."

"We wanted you to have people there that look like you," Daddy said, "so we picked the temple that was a little farther away."

"What do you mean?" Ruby asked. She looked a little like Mama and Daddy, but she didn't look like Emma and Jenny. They weren't related or anything.

"When I was in Hebrew school," Daddy said, "I was the only brown kid in the whole school. Sometimes it made me feel lonely. I didn't want you to have to go through that too."

"I don't feel like that, Daddy."

Daddy smiled at her from across the table. "I'm glad, Ruby." Beside him, four-year-old Micah accidentally flipped the bowl with his peas all over the table.

That night, Daddy came to Ruby's room to say goodnight. He sat at the edge of the bed and asked, "Did you have any more questions about Hebrew school, Rubes?"

Ruby thought about it, tapping her finger to her chin. That made Daddy smile, and she loved making Daddy smile. "Why were you the only brown kid in your class?" she asked.

"Hmm. A lot of Jews in the US, we come from Europe. There are lots of other kinds of Jews too, but where I grew up, a lot of the Jews had family that came from Europe during the Second World War. Do you know what that is?" Ruby shook her head and Daddy said, "There was a big war in Europe and the government, they wanted to hurt the Jews. A lot of people died, but your great-great grandparents, they survived and they came here."

Ruby clutched her stuffed bear close to her chest. "Why would they want to hurt us?" she asked quietly.

"No good reason," Daddy said, frowning now. "But that's a very important thing to know about Judaism, Ruby. Whatever happens, we survive. We come from a legacy of survivors." He smoothed her hair back from her forehead. "Time for bed now."

"Can you tell me a bedtime story?" Ruby asked.

"Of course," Daddy said, coming to sit next to her. She scooted over and Daddy said, "Uncle Zane told me one once, when I had a sleepover with Miranda and Noah. Can I tell you that one?"

Ruby nodded, since she loved Zane, and Daddy started, "This is a story about death."

—

Ruby takes the hot dog, two packets of ketchup, and a glass of lemonade (she has to come back for the lemonade, actually, since her hands are full) and sits on one of the blankets on the grass. Her cousin-uncle-whatever Noah sits between her and Hallie, his daughter, and ruffles both their hair.

"How've you been, Ruby?"

"Good," she says between bites of hotdog. Across the blanket, Aunt Claire and Miranda's partner Bree chat with Hallie and Micah. Down a bit farther, Zane and Uncle Matt laugh at something Aunt Claire's daughter Sarah says. On Ruby's other side, Miranda pulls up a chair beside Henry.

Daddy sits down across from them. "How's work?" he asks Noah.

Boring adult stuff again. Ruby watches a ladybug crawl across the blanket for a minute before she hears Daddy say, "And Ruby's doing great in school. Right Ruby?"

She nods. "We're back in the classrooms," she says.

"Hallie too," Noah tells her. "She went back last year." Ruby nods because same and Noah asks, "Do you like being back?"

"Yeah, I like seeing my friends. I liked not having to get up so early though."

"Don't we all," Noah says. "I'm glad we get to see you."

Ruby nods. "Family is important," she says.

The adults laugh, but Ruby doesn't know what's so funny.

"Where'd you hear that, Rubes?" Noah asks.

"Mama," she says. She said it many years ago, after the family tree project, but Ruby remembers.

"Mama's right," Daddy says. "Family is important." He smiles at her, and Ruby smiles back. She loves when he smiles at her, like she's the most important person ever.

"For better or worse," Daddy says, "family is everything."

Acknowledgements

The stories in these pages are so personal and so emotional that I could not have gotten through this project alone. First, I have to thank Rachel for reading Kindergarten a billion years ago and thinking it might be worth something, even as a first draft and even after I took a years-long break. Plus, thank you for reading over Ruby's story and making sure I got that eight-year-old voice right (writing children is *so* difficult). And of course, for reading through the entire manuscript one more time before it went out into the world. You're my favorite reader as well as one of my favorite people, so thank you for all that you do.

To Allison, Cass, Jenna, and Penina for being this full manuscript's first readers when I finally had more than four thousand words. You all were a dream when it came to workshopping and I appreciate you all endlessly. I can't wait for all of you to publish your stories so we can make little sections on our bookshelves for all of our books. I'll need mine signed! TLDR; It means the world to have a group of people who support me and strive to make my writing better.

Thank you to Mylène for reading these stories not long after everyone else and giving me, as always, incredibly thoughtful advice. I value your feedback more than I can say. Thank you to Michelle, who of course had to read a draft before I officially submitted it. I'm so lucky to have you in my corner. To Leah and the other Allison, for dealing with me while I went through the ups and downs of working on this manuscript. Allison, especially, was excited about the Scarlett Witch reference in chapter six. Y'all are the best and I couldn't have done this without you both.

Of course, I would be remiss if I didn't thank David Watkins and Candida Lacey. David, for seeing something worthwhile in my words and Candida, for working with me tirelessly to put them out into the world. To Candida especially, it means so much to me that I have people willing to fight to have these stories told. I can never fully express to you the extent of my gratitude, but I hope this is a start.

This book required a lot of research, but I also wanted to hear firsthand from people with lived experiences that I do not share. I have to thank my sensitivity readers, Jamieson and Victoria, for sharing your stories and making this manuscript the best it could possibly be. To everyone at Vine Leaves Press, but especially Melanie, Jessica, and Amie, thank you for believing in my manuscript and putting so much work into making it shine. To my agent, Daniele, and everyone at M&O, it's an absolute dream to work with you. I'm so glad this is going to be our first published book together.

Thank you, last but not least, to you, the reader. Without you, we authors would just be shouting into the void. Thank you for hearing our stories.

Further Reading

Many of the organizations referenced in these stories are real organizations doing incredible work. Breaking the Silence is an organization comprised of ex-Israeli Defense Force soldiers working to expose the realities of what goes on in the military. Their ultimate goal is to bring an end to the Israeli occupation in Palestine. You can check out their work at breakingthesilence.org.il.

Likewise, Jewish Voice for Peace aims to build a "strong, resilient Jewish community beyond Zionism." Their goal is to create real policy changes in the US around Israel and Palestine. They were the first major Jewish group to demand an end to US military aid to Israel until the end of the occupation in Palestine and are currently the only to support Boycott, Divestment, and Sanctions, or BDS, a Palestinian movement to move away from Israeli goods. You can learn more at their website, jewishvoiceforpeace.org, and learn more about BDS at bdsmovement.net.

The shooting that claimed Helena Altenberg's life in the story is fictional, but there was a very real shooting that took place at the Tree of Life synagogue in Pittsburgh, Pennsylvania, on November 4, 2018. Eleven people died. Their names were Bernice and Sylvan Simon, Cecil and David Rosenthal, Daniel Stein, Irving Younger,

Jerry Rabinowitz, Joyce Fienberg, Melvin Wax, Richard Gottfried, and Rose Mallinger.

There is no one Jewish experience, nor a "right way" to be Jewish. All of the characters throughout this book have a different relationship to their Judaism and the way it intersects with their various identities, such as any disabilities or mental health conditions, their gender, their race, their sexualities, and more. Likewise, there is no one way to be disabled, to struggle with mental health, to be queer, etc. All experiences and identities are valid.

For more reading about World War II and the Jewish experience, check out these books:

Sarah's Key by Tatiana de Rosnay
All The Light We Cannot See by Anthony Doerr
The Nightingale by Kristin Hannah
Number the Stars by Lois Lowry
The Alice Network by Kate Quinn
The Book Thief by Markus Zusak
Depart, Depart! by Sim Kern

Questions for Discussion

1. The first chapter opens with Gabi losing Eli, while the seventh chapter ends with their reunion. How does their relationship affect the rest of the events of the novel?

2. Some of the chapters feature unique stylistic choices, such as the spacing in chapter four, the use of second person in chapter six, and the use of present tense in the epilogue. Why do you think that is? Did you find these choices effective?

3. Storytelling is a big theme of this novel, such as the story Jason recalls in chapter two and the stories Zane tells his children in chapter three. Why do you think that is? What is a favorite story of yours and why?

4. The characters in this book all feel differently about Judaism; from Lena, who doesn't ever talk about it in adulthood, to Rebecca, who makes sure to take her children, and later her grandson, to temple. Do you think about religion often? Did you relate to any of these character's thoughts about religion?

5. Miranda advocates for a free Palestine against her family's wishes, specifically her grandparents. When was the last time you advocated for something you believed in? Did you have your family's support?

6. In the last line of the book, Jason tells Ruby, "Family is everything." Do you agree? Why might the author have chosen to close the book this way?

Vine Leaves Press

Enjoyed this book?
Go to *vineleavespress.com* to find more.
Subscribe to our newsletter:

9 783988 321183